THE GROWING ROCK

by

Susanna Lancaster

Harvard Square Editions
www.harvardsquareeditions.org
New York
2017

The Growing Rock, Susanna Lancaster

Copyright © 2017 by Susanna Lancaster

ISBN 978-1-941861-47-9
Printed in the United States of America

Cover design © Jeff Guy

Publisher's Note: This is a work of fiction. Names, characters,
places, and incidents are a product of the author's imagination.
Locales and public names are sometimes used for atmospheric
purposes. Any resemblance to actual people, living or dead, or
to businesses, companies, events, institutions, or locales
is completely coincidental.

Published in the United States by Harvard Square Editions
www.harvardsquareeditions.org

Praise for *The Growing Rock*

"For readers ages 10-14, *The Growing Rock* is a coming of age story which offers a realistic glimpse into life during the Depression. Caroline is an historically accurate character from a more innocent time. Particularly relatable for today's young readers is her relationship with Blanche, whom Caroline admires despite her selfish behavior. Also of particular tenderness is the budding romance between Caroline and Peter, the boy next door."

—The Historical Novel Society

"When I was a little girl I was obsessed with anything *Little House on the Prairie* and anything from that time period or setting because it was such a great series for children to grow up with. I read everything I could about that region and then slowly grew out of that phase. I never realized how much I would enjoy revisiting a book that could very easily fit into my favorite childhood genre, even though they are definitely set in different time periods. And I never thought I'd read a book that would make me want to read *Little Women* so much. But this book did! Not only was it a wave of nostalgia for me, it was a very incredible book to read. The characters were developed so well without it feeling drawn out."

—Paiges of a Book

"While this book contains just 200 pages, it feels like a lot more, in a positive way...it gave me the feeling of *The Little House on the Priarie,* and the book left me feeling nostalgic!"

—The Dutch Book Reviewer

To my husband, Kyle,
for telling me to keep going
when I didn't think I could.

"I never knew how much
like heaven this world could be,
when two people love
and live for one another!"

—*Little Women*, Louisa May Alcott

The Growing Rock
A Fairy Tale, By Caroline Neal, Grade 7

Once, there was a huge, gray rock that grew a little bit each year. Most people thought this was silly. Humans grow, animals grow, and plants grow. But how can a rock grow? After all, rocks don t eat, rocks do not sleep, and rocks do not have feelings.

The family whose land the rock rested on used it as a place to put their folded laundry when they took items off their clothes line. They ate on it when they had picnics. They sat on it at night and told stories and gazed at the stars. The rock sparkled in the sunlight and trapped in heat during the summertime. It stood as a castle in the midst of a sea of cotton in the autumn. It glistened in the snow and froze like a pond during the winter.

And, somehow, it grew.

I ve heard that it grows because there aren t any ants or worms below it. Instead, fairies live beneath it, a huge family of them. Hundreds upon hundreds of fairies. These fairies sleep all during the fall and winter, but near the end of spring, more fairies are born. They come out from underneath this rock at night and shine their glowing undersides in the darkness, like lightning bugs, and sprinkle their magical dust on children to make them grow. Thats why children in the family seem to grow so much more during the summer. It is when the Growing Rock grows it has to in order to make room for all the new fairies.

If you took a picture of this rock at the end of every summer, you might see a differance.

It is a small differance.

But it is definitely there.

Chapter 1

"Look, just hop on over. No one will notice." Caroline's older brother George clung onto the back of the giant fence, grinning down at her in that irresistible, up-to-no-good way that always got them in trouble.

She shook her head. *"I don't know."*

"Ahh, whatever. Suit yourself then." George swung one leg over, then the other, and disappeared into the darkness.

Caroline pressed her head against the fence. It was too hard to see through the cracks between the wood. Surely he was waiting on her, though. Surely he wouldn't really go off without her.

One thing was for sure—he was either waiting on her, or he moved with absolutely no noise like one of Miss Evelyn's cats because there was no shuffle behind that fence. That stupid fence. It was the only thing separating her from doing nothing or having the best time of her life. A few hundred feet away, people were laughing and dancing. Popped corn and sweet cakes filled the air. George had worn his best trousers and Sunday shoes to impress some girl named Sally Jo. Their sister Blanche would be there with her date. Maybe if Caroline went, someone would ask her to dance, too.

Just one fence. And sneaking in without paying.

"George," she called, *"Wait! I think I'm coming!"*

"Shush your loud mouth." So he had been waiting after all.

"Here, I'll help you," he said in a softer tone. His blonde head appeared over the fence.

He stuck out a hand, callused from long hours of chopping cotton. Caroline clung to it with both of her small hands. A moment later, she was over and they were walking fast, joining the crowd and trying to blend in.

It was hard to see the wooden dance floor. Bodies, slender ones and large ones, moved everywhere. They twirled so fast it didn't hardly matter that most of them wore the same outfits from the year before and the year before that. Every now and then, there was a new ivy cap proudly sitting on someone's head or some fresh, dainty gloves waving in the air. Suit jackets with an added pocket or two. Day dresses with a new bow. Sleeves that had been made puffier to drown the occasional waist that wasn't as slim as last summer. For the most part, though, the clothes felt as familiar as the people who wore them.

A guy who was only a couple of grades ahead in school blew into a clarinet and played everyone's favorite Benny Goodman song, "Let's Dance." Large pimples scattered his shiny face, and every time his cheeks filled with air, it seemed as if they would suddenly burst.

Caroline tapped her foot. Maybe George would dance a song or two with her. Except where had he gone? Maybe he'd found the girl he was looking for.

Someone bumped into her and almost knocked her down.

"Oh, hey, kiddo. How's it going?" It was Robert, Blanche's latest boyfriend.

Caroline rubbed her shoulder and grinned. Though half the jokester, Robert was George's best friend and had felt like a third older brother for years already. He'd lasted a whole year, which was about ten months longer than most of Blanche's love interests. If George didn't come back, Robert would dance with her.

"Well, George got me away from the Tomato Festival. So I'd say not too bad."

"That brother of yours—he sure knows how to get what he wants." Robert chuckled. "I finally got your sister away too. I'm glad this was her last year to be in that blasted pageant. Thought for sure these men on the front row wouldn't take no for an answer." He fanned his shiny face and pulled on his suspenders. "Lord, it's so hot."

Caroline nodded. Even in the night, it was probably eighty-five degrees or more. "Do you wanna dan—"

"Bobby Larry, why you stop it, you!" Blanche squealed from across the tent. She stood around a circle of friends, holding up a small silver crown for everyone to admire. It made six years in a row she'd been named the

Tomato Queen at the festival. Every year since she'd been old enough to enter the contest, she'd won. And it was no wonder why she kept winning. She wore the new red dress she'd talked Mama into making, and it fit her tiny waist perfectly. It dipped at the neckline just enough to show off the tops of her large bosom. She shook her auburn curls and, with a laugh, shooed away a man who kept standing too close.

"Now, Bobby Larry, what have I told you? You gotta wait your turn with all the other fellas if you want to dance."

A shadow passed over Robert's face for a second, but then he shook his head and laughed. "I better go before someone takes my woman. See ya later, kiddo." He hurried over to join the group.

Caroline groaned and walked away before Blanche could spot her. She probably wouldn't tattle to their parents, but who knew with Blanche? It would be dumb to risk it.

To go home and have Mama and Papa mad at her for sneaking away and running off where she wasn't supposed to be was the last thing she needed. What was she doing here anyway? No one would ask her to dance. She wasn't like Blanche. She wasn't pretty or popular. Mama had never even mentioned her entering The Tomato Queen contest, though if anyone looked like a tomato, it was Caroline with her strawberry blond hair and sunburned face. She'd just turned thirteen, but she looked much younger because she was so darn skinny.

She left the tent and ran past the colorful booths of prizes and candy. "George?" she called. "George, where are you?"

Her forehead felt wet and greasy with the combination of sweat and the makeup Aunt June let her borrow.

"George?"

"Shhh," George said out of nowhere, stepping out from behind a stack of barrels. He handed her a cotton candy. "I told you to be quiet. If anyone asks you, you dropped your ticket when you rode on the Ferris wheel."

"But I didn't ride on the Ferris wheel. I don't even have a— "

"Shhh," George stuffed a piece of cotton candy in her mouth. It tasted light and sweet. Caroline didn't even have to chew it. It just kind of melted on its own.

George popped a piece in his own mouth. He grinned. "Relax, sis. Have some fun. God knows we need it after working in those doggone fields all day."

"Where's Sally Jo? Did you find her yet?"

"You know, this town's too small for me." Maybe it was the lighting, but his blue eyes looked shiny.

"What do you mean?" Caroline tore another chunk of cotton candy and let it rest on her tongue a minute.

"Exactly what I said. It's too small. Same thing day after day. Same people we've always known. The same handful of pretty girls, always gettin' taken by the same handful of fellas, the ones who have more money." He started toward the Ferris wheel. Caroline had to walk fast to keep up.

The Ferris wheel looked huge against the starry sky. Its lighted booths spun round and round.

"Nah, I belong somewhere else, sis. You and I both do. We're not like the others around here."

Caroline bumped into George. "What? Why'd you stop?"

"Forget it. Let's just get out of here," he said. His tongue looked bright pink from the cotton candy in the colorful lights.

A pretty redhead in a simple homespun dress who must've been Sally Jo stood waiting in line with a tall boy who was holding a stuffed bear he must've won for her. Sally Jo looked in their direction. Her face turned red, and she looked the other way.

"What do you say we get out of here?"

Caroline nodded.

Once they slipped past the crowd, they raced toward the fence, laughing and tripping in the dark. George jumped over, and then Caroline, landing in his arms and almost knocking him down.

George threw her on his shoulders, the way he had when she was younger, and ran again. "You're so light, I can barely feel you," he joked.

The wind blew Caroline's hair away from her face. The air felt refreshing against her sunburn, like a splash of water.

He was right. They were alike. They were the only two not dancing.

Right then, for just a moment, it felt more as if they were flying.

Chapter 2

"Caroline, snap out of it," Aunt Elsmere said, "Hand me that ribbon."

Caroline shook her head. She handed her the green ribbon beside her.

"Not that one. The red one. Really, child. Blanche is wearing a red dress. Pay more attention." The red ribbon almost perfectly matched Aunt Elsmere's flushed, round face.

Caroline sighed.

It didn't seem like it'd been a year ago since they'd snuck into the Bisbee Show. She'd been so worried about getting caught at first, but then the thought never returned once she'd gotten in. It was always like that when George was around. Safe. It was hard to stay worried when he was so carefree and reassuring. He had a joke for everything.

This year Caroline was stuck going to the Tomato Festival once again. It was fun when she was Phoebe's age, but now it seemed pointless. The same nasty tomatoes, the same old boring red dresses with different trimming to make them look new, even though everyone knew everyone was too poor to afford new clothes.

The kitchen was crowded and hot with everybody stuffed in there measuring and trying on dresses. They'd kept the curtains drawn most of the day, but it hadn't helped much.

Blanche stood still while Mama and Aunt Elsmere worked on the red dress she'd worn the year before. Phoebe, now seven years old, but still the size of a five-year-old, stood on one of the kitchen chairs with her arms held out to the sides. Aunt June hovered around her with pins poking from the side of her mouth.

Caroline fanned her face. It felt good to have that silly dress off and to wear nothing but her underclothes.

"Caroline, do put your dress back on," Aunt Elsmere snapped. She walked toward her and put the chicken-feed sack dress back over her head. It still had a salty stench from when she'd worked earlier. Caroline pulled it down and slipped her arms through the arm holes. Already she could feel more moisture forming on her skin. Her armpits started sticking to the damp sleeves.

Papa came in from the cotton fields at just the right moment. "My, how lovely my girls look."

Caroline grinned. Papa was a good liar. Not all the time, of course, but he could tell a fib from there to Nashville when a room was getting steamed up and Aunt Elsmere was being a pain.

Then again, what he said wasn't completely untrue. Blanche twirled around in the red dress she and Mama had fussed about all afternoon. It fit her tiny frame perfectly and made her chest look bigger than normal. With her dark hair, she looked good in red. Which was why she wore it all the time to match her red lipstick. Blanche could wear a cotton sack and still look pretty.

The same couldn't be said about Caroline. She had to be careful about the colors she wore. Her strawberry blonde hair just didn't go with pinks, oranges, or reds.

Phoebe didn't look much better. She tried to copy Blanche, twirling until you could see her undies. Caroline hoped that soon Phoebe could get a new dress. Her red dress was way too short, almost like the ones Shirley Temple wore in the pictures, only Shirley had sweet, soft legs with dimples. Phoebe's were so thin her knee caps stuck out sharply, like knots on the old oak in the side yard.

"Why don't you ladies go on outside where it's cooler?" Papa poured a glass of water from the pitcher beside the stove and winked at Aunt June.

Aunt June must have understood. She always seemed to understand her older brother, the same way Caroline understood George. Papa's look said he was tired and didn't want to hear any more about dresses.

"Fantastic idea," Aunt June said, fanning her flushed face.

Mama walked Phoebe upstairs for a nap. Then she joined the rest of them outside.

Everyone except Caroline. There was no point going outside with them. Not when it was just the women. They'd change the topic the minute she'd walk away, and they'd hush or just stop talking altogether if she came back. Aunt Elsmere would stare at her up and down, debating whether she was finally old enough to be considered a "woman."

Papa closed the screened door to the back porch and adjusted the straps of the suspenders on his overalls and sat down in one of the kitchen chairs. It instantly felt hotter with the door closed.

"How's it going, sweetpea?" Papa slowly pulled off one of his boots. His sock came out all damp looking.

"I finished planting seeds in that area of the south side of the cotton field," Caroline said. "Before I had to come inside for these stupid dresses."

Papa smiled, and his blue eyes twinkled. "That's my girl." He loosened the collar on his shirt, also soaking wet. He poured some more water. When Caroline drew it from the well half an hour before, it had been cold, but by now it was fairly warm.

Papa didn't seem to mind if it was hot, though. He emptied the glass with one swallow and poured another one.

Caroline sat down and leaned against the smooth, yellow and cream striped wallpaper.

The tiled flooring felt cool against her legs. It was too bad she couldn't take the dirty dress off and sit there in her slip again.

Aunt June's whisper came from the back porch. Somehow when she tried speaking softly, her voice carried even louder than normal.

But maybe she meant to talk loud so Caroline *could* hear. She usually repeated everything later anyhow and they'd have a good laugh over it.

"Well, as I'm always sayin'," Aunt June said, "If ya eat the right things, like pickles and such, you can avoid crampin' every month."

"Now, come here, you know that's not true," Aunt Elsmere argued. "Nothin' works like chopped onion."

Mama's thin frame was visible through the screened-in doorway. She rocked back and forth in her white, whicker rocking chair, sipping on a glass of water and fanning her flushed forehead. Her hair was tied in its usual knot at the nape of her neck.

It was a shame she never wore it down because in the bedroom upstairs there was a picture of her on her wedding day, and her golden hair had been pretty and curly, just like Phoebe's. Papa had been leaving for the war shortly after that, but they smiled as if nothing could get through to their happiness. Now, Mama looked cross with her hair pulled back so tight.

But Papa stared at her from across the room, as if she looked exactly like the young girl in the photo.

"Shh," Mama whispered. "Y'all can discuss *that* all you want to, when Caroline or Phoebe aren't where they may happen to listen."

"Mama, Phoebe's asleep, and Caroline's fourteen now."

Mama's figure blocked Blanche's face, but it was just like Blanche to roll her eyes as she said this. It was easy to tell she had by the way her voice went up a notch.

Mama frowned. "Fourteen isn't that old."

Blanche giggled. "I'm not much older, and look at the difference. When I was her age, I had Billy John and David and Eugene asking me to dances and picture shows."

Caroline held her breath. Sometimes Blanche's teasing and talking down upon her worked in her favor. Maybe Mama would change her mind and let her go to the Bisbee Show after all. She usually listened to Blanche.

But Caroline didn't hear Mama's response.

Papa laughed. "Those ladies are something else. Let's go sit on the front porch. It's shadier there." He pulled his wet hat off. A red band shone around the top of his forehead from where he'd worn it all day. He poured more water in his glass. Then he gave a second one to her.

Caroline followed Papa outside and sat on the swing, but she scooted away from him. She probably didn't smell too good herself, but the odor from his sweat nearly made her gag.

She took a sip of the lukewarm water and breathed deeply. At least with the sun facing the opposite side of the house, the air was finally starting to cool down somewhat. Papa whistled his favorite hymn, "His Eye is on the Sparrow."

Caroline leaned her head against the back of the swing. Her eyes closed. Soon she'd have to go inside and help prepare supper, but right now she wanted to sit there and listen to Papa's whistling.

Her eyes opened. Papa had stopped whistling and swinging. Now the only sound was the crickets' early evening chirp.

"I worry about Phoebe," he said all of a sudden. "None of y'all took so many naps when you was her age."

It was hard remembering that far back. Everything was different when she'd been seven.

There hadn't been as much to worry about. But things were harder for Phoebe. She'd almost died from pneumonia a few months before. Who cared if she napped a lot now?

But Papa looked worried.

Caroline scratched her legs. They were covered in mosquito bites. A bloody bite on her right foot had dried and looked as if a grape had been smudged on it.

Papa sighed. "I'm gonna miss this place."

Caroline's fingernails accidentally ripped the scab off. What was Papa saying?

"Caroline, I know you don't want to hear this, but I think I've got to try something else for a little while. With your brothers no longer living here, we need more help, but we can't afford it. I think I may test my luck in Memphis, or maybe go up more north. Just to find some work to help get us through."

Caroline's heart pounded. It was a wonder Papa didn't hear it.

"If I go, will you promise me you'll look after Phoebe like you helped your Mama do before?"

Her mind raced so fast it was hard to answer. Lots of children had stopped coming to school to help their families. So many people had started selling off their land and animals because they couldn't afford hired help anymore, or weren't selling their crops like they used to. Parents of families who lived in town came home every day to say they'd lost their jobs and had to move to a larger city.

It was sad, but simple. People who weren't lucky enough to grow their food the way Caroline's family did couldn't afford to eat. It was normal to hear about other families' problems all the time, but *they* always managed. Somehow.

"We've got to get more mules before harvest." Papa sighed. "And, of course, we need to know about George."

Caroline nodded and scratched her foot again.

George had left after Christmas to find work somewhere else when both of the old mules died within several weeks of each other. He'd helped out a lot at first with bits of money here and there. All of a sudden, though, his letters stopped. They'd already used the money he'd sent to pay for medicine for Phoebe.

Most people in the family thought he'd been killed during all the Ohio and Mississippi River floods that happened around the same time. After all, it wasn't like him to forget his family. And it was odd that no one had seen him. Even Aunt Elsmere, who came to live with them when her own home was flooded, hadn't seen him since he stayed a couple of nights in Kentucky with her.

But George couldn't be gone. Of the five kids in the family, he was probably the strongest of them all. Hardly got sick, and when he did, he wasn't cooped up very long. The thought of his smiling face and familiar blue Neal eyes felt so real, it seemed as if he were still there. And he probably would be back soon, so what was the point in Papa leaving too?

Besides, if they were already struggling like Papa said, they'd never make it with him gone. They'd never be able to chop the cotton on their own all summer and have it ready to pick in autumn. They'd end up at one of those soup kitchens that poor people in the cities went to. Phoebe would never get to begin school in the fall. She'd have to pick cotton, if they had any worth picking. Caroline would never graduate high school. On the farm next to theirs, Peter would finish school and go on to be a doctor the way he'd always talked about, while she'd be stuck in Ripley, never passing, or even starting, the ninth grade.

Papa's strong arm wrapped around her shoulder. He wiped her face with the handkerchief he kept in his front pocket.

Papa's bad smell no longer mattered. Caroline leaned against him. Tears streamed from her eyes and trickled down her neck and underneath her dress, cool against her grimy skin.

Inside, Blanche and Aunt June were starting supper, clanging pots around and joking.

"Sweetpea, please don't give me that look," Papa said. "I've got to count on you. I've already talked to Peter's family, and they're going to help y'all if we share some of our crops. And, of course, Aunt June and Uncle P. Joe are just up the road. Thomas and Pamelia are only a few miles from here."

The tears continued. The drops on Caroline's chest made her shiver, despite how hot it was. The delicate hairs on her arms stood up.

"You'll at least get to have your friend Peter around more. You'll have more time to be kids and have fun while school's out."

Caroline groaned. Again, Papa was a good liar. The way he talked made her want to believe him, but she knew better. Of course they wouldn't have time for anything else besides chopping cotton and tending to the vegetable garden. He knew that, so why make it sound better than it actually was?

"Why can't I go with you? Or go instead?"

"I know you would if I let you, but I'm afraid you're not old enough. Not much work for a young girl like you."

Caroline crossed her arms. "If someone told Amelia Earhart that and she listened, she'd never have stepped foot on a plane."

Papa chuckled softly. "You're probably right. But for now, I need you at home to keep an eye on things, just until I'm back. I need you to be like those girls in that book of yours. Y'all need to look out for each other, the way they did when their father was at war."

Papa was talking about *Little Women*, one of the few books she owned. Caroline got Phoebe to act it out with her all the time. She could quote chapters of it word for word. If she compared the situation to that book, maybe it wouldn't be so bad. And this time, Papa wasn't leaving to go to war. That was all over before she was even born, and the world would probably never go to war like that again. Papa was just going to find work.

But then it was as if the life she knew were a flame being blown out that couldn't ever be re-lit. George had told her something very similar not long ago.

Then he disappeared.

The next morning, the family sat on the porch waiting. Waiting for the sun to rise higher. Waiting for the day to grow hotter. Waiting for their family to be separated more.

Charles Jackson was coming to pick Papa up and give him a ride to the nearest train station. He was one of their few friends in Ripley who owned a car.

Even though the sun was barely up, it was already baking everything. It would be another unbearable day in the cotton fields. But Phoebe was wrapped in a blanket and snuggled in Papa's lap, as if it were winter. She slept soundly, not aware that he was leaving, perhaps, forever, just like George.

Blanche sat beside Caroline on the top step. She didn't look at Caroline, but when their knees touched, she didn't bother moving away. A long time ago, they would've held hands during something like that. Blanche would've said everything would be okay and given Caroline a hug.

But they were older now.

Blanche's face was pale. She twirled a strand of auburn hair around her index finger.

Was she also worried that Papa wouldn't come back?

Blanche and George had always been paired up in the fields together, had always been close—they were hardly even a year apart in age. When he disappeared, she hadn't gone out with friends for a month. A long time for her. Then she got moody and angry all the time. What would she be like if Papa didn't come back?

Mama leaned on Papa's shoulder, her bun loose for once. Her large eyes looked off into the distance at the still pink and orange sunrise, but they stared aimlessly, as if not really seeing. She looked *almost* pretty again, like she had been in that wedding photo.

Papa stared at the top of Phoebe's curly head. A tear escaped the corner of his left eye. He looked more tired than he had the night before, after working all day. Wrinkles lined his face, and streaks of gray seemed to pop out of his stubble in the early light.

No one said anything.

Suddenly, Blanche pointed at a speck in the distance that was Charles Jackson's old Model T coming along the dirt road. They could see it moving in the openness and growing larger until it was parked right in front of them.

Phoebe woke up and smiled at the surprise. Charles Jackson had given them a ride home from church once.

"Are we gonna go somewhere? Can I honk the horn?"

"Not today, sweetie." Papa kissed the top of Phoebe's head and stood up and placed her in Caroline's lap.

The weight of everything came down on Caroline with a suddenness.

Papa was really leaving.

Charles Jackson helped Papa put his few belongings into the back of the car. Its rear had been removed a long time ago to turn it into a pickup. In the fall, farmers sometimes paid Charles to haul their cotton bales that would be shipped on boats to the Memphis Cotton Exchange. Caroline's family had done so many times when the mules got too old and weak to make the trips.

It made no sense, then, why Charles was driving Papa when they already owed him for work done months ago, before

George had even left. Either Uncle P. Joe and Aunt June had paid him behind their backs again, or Charles had a crush on Blanche.

Papa hugged each of them good-bye. He patted the top of Caroline's head. "Be strong for me, sweetpea," he whispered.

Phoebe started crying. "Don't leave, Daddy! Don't go!"

Caroline choked back the tears that threatened to escape. She'd have a good cry later, in the fields, or in her room. But not now. Not in front of Phoebe.

"Shh," she whispered in Phoebe's ear. "It will all be okay."

Blanche gave in and leaned over and put an arm around Caroline and Phoebe. She looked as if she was trying not to cry, too.

Mama walked to the car with Papa. She handed him a basket with cornbread and jam and a great big baked potato that would be his dinner a few hours later. They kissed good-bye. When Mama turned around, she looked years older. She wouldn't say a word, but worry was all over her face.

Charles Jackson cranked the engine. A moment later, the Model T was once more nothing but a speck in the distance, leaving a small dust of clouds behind.

Another moment and Papa was gone.

Chapter 3

Caroline dug the garden spade into the earth and pulled out a long weed. She tossed it in a basket full of others she had picked that morning and took a deep breath.

The sun shone directly above the small, white house. The front porch was fully exposed to the parching rays of light. Not a cloud in the sky.

It had to be at least one o'clock. And at least ninety degrees already.

She fanned herself with her less dirty hand. Too bad she'd forgotten to wear a hat. The part in her hair that separated her plaited pigtails itched already. She'd have a fresh red line of sunburn tracing her scalp at the end of the day for sure. But it was easy to put off going inside and getting Papa's big hat each time she pulled another weed. It was worth avoiding everyone—Blanche whining about nothing to wear and Aunt Elsmere's nagging.

Worst of all was Mama. How could she just let Papa go? Then act strange and quiet, not talking much to anyone.

Caroline kicked the basket of weeds. How could Papa do this?

"Caroline! You need to come inside for dinner."

Phoebe's blonde head bobbed above the rows of tomatoes and moved toward her.

"Where are you?"

"I'm over here." Caroline jumped up so Phoebe could spot her behind the wire tomato cages. Suddenly, she stood beside her.

"What is it?"

"Mommy wants you to come inside. She said it's hot, and you need to eat."

Caroline groaned. Being in the heat long enough made her lose her appetite. It made her forget everything.

Phoebe looked up at her, waiting for an answer. She smiled and revealed a toothy grin in which her top front teeth were missing.

Caroline's head was heavy from the heat. She felt dizzy, everything blurry. Papa's words from a few nights before came back so clear that for a second it seemed as if he was there.

"Oh, all right." She wiped her hands on the thin, cotton dress that was getting too short. She didn't bother picking up the basket. She shook her head to knock off the dizziness and smiled back at Phoebe. "Race you to the house."

"Okay, but I'll win." Phoebe started to run as fast as her short legs would carry her.

Caroline let her get a head start. Racing was Phoebe's favorite game. Papa said it was good for Phoebe and would help her skinny legs develop some muscles, so Caroline almost always let her win.

When they stumbled through the kitchen door, Mama was sewing a piece of lace on one of her old dresses. It was a soft lilac that was one of the few nice things she still had from when she was a girl.

Blanche glanced up from the table with her eyes looking red and puffy, as if she'd been crying. Maybe she couldn't stop thinking about Papa either.

Caroline walked over and put her hand on her sister's shoulder. "I miss him too," she said.

"What?" Blanche asked.

"Papa."

Blanche shook her head and picked up the other end of the dress, as if she hadn't heard her. "I wore this thing for the first time three years ago," she mumbled.

Was Blanche joking? How could she worry about a silly dress? Had she not seen how awful Papa looked the morning he left?

Caroline turned away and washed an apple for Phoebe in the large and dinted tin basin below the kitchen window.

"I don't know why I can't just get a new one from Berg and Schaeffer's. I wore that on all my dates with Eugene two years ago," Blanche continued. "What if everyone else has something new and I'm the only one wearing the same old thing? Or worse, what if Eugene is there and recognizes it? You know, he got married last month."

"Poor dear, 'wearing the same old thing.' That's much worse than losing your home in a flood like Aunt Elsmere, or having to sell everything you own like the Browns did." Caroline frowned and took one of the cold ham and cheese sandwiches made on corn bread. Each one was cut into four small triangles so it lasted longer.

"Oh, hush," Blanche said. "You're just jealous cause you ain't ever going anywhere.

No one's ever gonna ask you. I mean, just look at yourself. You're as red as one of them tomatoes you've been pickin'.'"

The blood rushed to Caroline's face. That might have been true, but Blanche had no right saying so. And why was she making Mama fix another dress when she looked so perfect in the red one she wore to the Bisbee Show every year anyhow?

"At least I don't just sit inside all damn day. Not lazy like you," Caroline snapped back in a low enough tone so Mama didn't catch her cursing.

Blanche clenched her teeth. She was one of several in the Ripley High's class of 1937 who hadn't graduated. It wasn't because she *had* to stop going to school to work and help pay for bills, though; it was because she'd gotten engaged and decided in December that she didn't *need* any more education.

"Girls," Mama said, "That's quite enough. Phoebe's eating and minding her own business. Now why can't you? Your father's only been gone a few days, and here you are already causing trouble."

"Well, *I* wouldn't be arguing if we had one decent piece of material in this house."

Blanche looked at the floor and lowered her voice. "Or if Robert could just get a real job and buy a house so we could be married already."

"Well, *I* wouldn't be arguing if someone would help with all the work today. Papa leaves, so y'all just act like you're on some damn vacation," Caroline snapped back.

"That's enough!" Mama set the dress down and put her forehead in her hands. She looked up, her face pale. "Both of you, stop it. Blanche, I'll have the dress done soon as I can, but not if you keep acting like this. And, Caroline, you better watch your language. And don't you go a thinkin' you're the only one getting things done. I've already hoed the vegetable garden before you were even awake. P. Joe and Thomas came over a couple of hours ago to do some cotton planting, even though Thomas should have been at home with Pamelia cause she's been sick again. You didn't know any of that. You just complained and felt sorry for yourself."

Blanche gave her a knowing smirk.

Caroline put her fourth of a sandwich down. She grabbed Papa's work hat and went back outside.

The ground was so dry it seemed pointless to put more seeds in the ground. But Caroline did anyway. She stood up from her bent position, her back aching something awful.

They'd never taken so long to plant cotton before. Normally, it was all finished by March or April. They'd get it done quickly with their hired help. This year, they'd planted in spurts, with only some people doing the work and without much additional help.

Beads of moisture dripped down into her eyes as she stared at the ground that would eventually be a sea of whiteness around her. She wiped her forehead on the back of her hand.

The wind blew for a moment. If the cotton were there, it would have been twirling like snow. It was the only breeze she'd felt all day. If a breeze like that continued, maybe it wouldn't be so bad.

Blanche walked toward her and set her sack of seeds down. "You reckon we did enough for today?"

Caroline grinned. The heat either put Blanche in a bad mood, or it made her forget she was supposed to be in a bad mood and not talking to her.

"Well, Mama told us just to do as much as we could. Uncle P. Joe's gonna help finish the last bit tomorrow, and Thomas—if Pamelia isn't still sick. And Peter." As Blanche said this last name, Caroline's face turned red. It didn't make sense, but for some reason she felt different around Peter lately. She hoped Blanche hadn't noticed.

Blanche didn't. She shaded her eyes. "Then what do ya say we call it quits and take a lemonade break?"

"Sounds good to me."

They walked in silence back to the house. Caroline's vision blurred again like it had that morning. She stumbled. Blanche grabbed Caroline's sack of seeds and carried them in one hand and hers in the other.

Blanche studied her. "Your face is awful pale, Caroline. Sit under that huge oak and rest a minute. I'll bring out some drinks."

Caroline did as she was told. Her head felt heavy as she leaned it against the tree trunk.

A moment later, Blanche returned with a couple of sugar cookies tied in a cloth napkin and two glasses of lemonade.

Caroline squinted, even in the shade. Mama never let them have sweets in the middle of the day.

Blanche read her thoughts. "I know. But she didn't care. She said you needed to eat proper, and she doesn't give a hoot what it is, so long's you eat something."

That wasn't like Mama. It seemed as if since Papa left, she hadn't cared much about anything.

Caroline shrugged and unfolded the napkin. She nibbled on the cookie to make it last longer. It was soft and delicious and made her feel much better after she finished it. She sipped the lemonade, sweet and sour but not very cold.

"Wish ole Larry's ice truck would drive by today. I'd give a dime for some ice on a day like today."

"If you had a dime," Blanche corrected her.

True. If Caroline had a dime, she could afford The Bisbee Show. But, of course, she didn't have the money, especially now that Papa was gone.

Blanche's fiancé didn't really have the money either. What little Robert did have he could barely save for the wedding because Blanche would insist on going to the town square every weekend and doing everything fun that came along.

Caroline lay all the way back. In the shade, with a stomach no longer growling, she could almost fall asleep. George used to take a nap every day. He could sleep anywhere.

Blanche leaned back also, her dark hair blending in a little bit with the tree trunk, and she stared up at the branches, hardly blinking.

Was she thinking about George too? Was she also reminded of the picnics they'd had under that same tree? Or how picking cotton was always fun with him throwing it at them, as if it were snowballs?

Caroline sighed. "Blanche, do you think George is coming back?"

Blanche snapped out of her trance. She clenched her teeth. "We've been through this already. George would never just drop us like this. So, no, I don't think he is. We would've heard from him by now."

"But you don't think he's—you know—dead—do you?"

Blanche's eyes watered. "Yes, yes, I do. Or something really bad has happened cause we would've heard something by now."

George's round, tanned face with his blue eyes that always twinkled just like Papa's and smile that could make anyone feel better flashed before Caroline's eyes. His loud laugh echoed in her mind. How could he possibly be dead? Someone so young and confident? Someone who could take the worse situation and make a joke out of it? No, he couldn't possibly be gone.

"Well, I don't think that for a second. And Mama and Papa have sent letters to everyone we know asking if they've heard anything. I bet we'll hear back real quick."

Blanche poured the rest of her lemonade in the grass and stood up. "So he's okay and just ignores us this long? You know how bad all those floods were. They *ruined* Aunt Elsmere's home. They *killed* hundreds of people. He wouldn't have stood a chance." Without waiting for an answer, she turned around and walked into the house.

Past the barn and the vegetable gardens, the empty field lay as still as ever, like a thick blanket of snow in the wintertime, only it was broken and turned brown with little greenness. Caroline was cold all of a sudden.

She heard George laughing and felt his arms gently push her thin shoulders, just like the last time they went sledding.

The last day she saw him.

"It's burst into flames! It's burst into flames and its falling and crashing!"

Phoebe cried and squeezed Mama around the neck. Aunt Elsmere kept shaking and put her head in her hands. The radio reporter's voice pierced through the room, the way Papa used a knife to butcher a pig.

An airship had caught fire and crashed the day before.

"It's just laying there, mass of smoking wreckage," said the voice. "Ah! And everybody can hardly breathe and talk and the screaming—"

Caroline held her breath.

Phoebe cried more.

"Turn that damn radio off," Blanche finally snapped from where she sat in the corner of the room.

"Don't use that kinda language in this house," Mama fussed.

Blanche slammed her copy of *Gone with the Wind* down on the end table and nearly knocked over the kerosene lamp. She walked over to the radio and turned it off.

Aunt Elsmere grunted. "Might as well just take the batteries out, while you're at it."

Blanche glared and went upstairs. Caroline sighed. She and Phoebe would have to wait a while now before they could go to bed. Blanche would need at least a good half hour to cool down. She was still mad from talking about George earlier. Any mention of death was sure to set her off. And the radio reporter was talking about lots of deaths. Thirty-five of them, to be exact.

"Guess that probably wasn't the best thing for the children to hear," Mama muttered, wiping Phoebe's face.

"No, I'd say not," Aunt Elsmere agreed. She turned to Caroline with that quizzing look in her eyes. "Do you even *know* what an airship is?"

Mama's jaw tightened. She picked up the basket of clothes she was mending. "Their understanding wasn't really what I meant. I think I may just go on up to bed."

Of course Mama had only meant it was too scary for them to hear, but Aunt Elsmere had to turn everything into some sort of test. Her gaze never faltered. "Well, do you?" she repeated.

"Umm—" Caroline had seen a picture of an aircraft before. Long and kinda oval-shaped like a balloon at The Bisbee Show. "Isn't it just like an airplane?"

"Wrong!" Aunt Elsmere boomed.

"Close enough," Mama snapped at Aunt Elsmere. "It's transportation in the sky. Only I think it's filled with gas or something."

Caroline and Phoebe gave each other knowing looks. Sometimes Mama and Aunt Elsmere could debate for days.

Phoebe looked as if she'd cry again when Mama started to walk away. It was almost completely dark, but the curtains and windows were still open to let the night air in. The trees cast eerie shadows on the plain wooden walls where the light from the lamp didn't quite reach.

It was still very hot, even without the sun.

"Mama," Caroline asked, "Can Phoebe and I sleep outside?"

Mama paused and turned around. She pulled a blanket from the top of the laundry basket and handed it to her. "Sure. Here, take this, and y'all can use the cot that's folded in the corner." She tilted her head toward Phoebe. "If she starts actin' sickly or gets cold, bring her inside, okay?"

Caroline nodded.

"And say a special prayer for those poor families who lost loved ones yesterday," Mama said. Her eyes watered, and she turned her head. She was thinking about George again.

Mama went upstairs. Caroline held Phoebe's hand and led the way to the back porch.

She set up the cot like Mama had said, and then they both lay down.

Being small didn't matter at the moment. It was nice that they could both still fit. Sharing a bed with Phoebe was much better than sharing the bed with Blanche. It was a lot cooler there too, and the mosquitos couldn't get through the thick screen.

They both lay on their sides and faced each other.

"Caroline?"

"Yes?"

"I miss Papa."

Caroline sighed. "I do too." It was hard to believe he'd only been gone a few days. It seemed as if he'd been gone for weeks already.

"Caroline?"

"Yes?"

"Do you think Papa died on that airplane? The one that exploded?" Phoebe's voice trembled.

"*The Hindenburg*? It's an aircraft. And, no, of course not. That happened yesterday. Papa spoke to Aunt June on the telephone yesterday. He couldn't have been on it. And, besides, why in the world would Papa fly anywhere anyway? The man said it caught fire in New Jersey. He's not going that far."

Phoebe shivered.

Caroline pulled the blanket up. "It's gonna be okay."

Phoebe was quiet for a minute.

"Caroline?"

"Yes?"

"Do you think George is coming back?"

She gulped. How could she answer that when she didn't know herself?

"I don't know," she whispered. "But I hope so. Guess that's really all we can do. That and say all of your prayers."

Phoebe sighed. "I miss him. And I miss Thomas."

"But Thomas didn't go nowhere! He just has his own house. He's married."

Phoebe frowned and pulled the thin blanket to her chin. Her hair was tangled around her face, and it was still almost white looking with the light from the moon streaming in through the screened-in walls.

"I hate stupid weddings," Phoebe said. "I don't want Blanche to get married."

Caroline laughed. It would probably be better once Blanche moved out. At least there would be less arguing.

Phoebe didn't say anything else for a few minutes. Caroline closed her eyes and was almost asleep.

"Caroline?" Phoebe whispered.

Caroline rubbed her eyes. "Yes?"

"Can you tell me a story? Can you tell me about the Growing Rock?"

Caroline smiled sleepily.

The Growing Rock was a large rock down the hill behind their house. When Caroline was younger, around Phoebe's age, George had told her that the rock was a growing one. She didn't think it could grow. How *could* a rock grow? But he insisted it did, and that it grew a little bit each summer. And she'd believed it. At the time, so had Blanche.

Before George left, a whole year ago, Caroline had written a small story about the Rock for school. She'd even typed it on the school typewriter. She'd won an award for it. After George went missing, she'd thrown the story in a trunk in the bedroom. She didn't want to look at it. It made her think of George.

But, somehow, it just never seemed fair not to tell the story to Phoebe, even if it made Caroline herself a little sad.

"What do you want to know about it? You already know everything."

Phoebe shook her head. The cot moved too. "Nuh-uh. Not everything. Who lives there?"

Caroline grinned. This was the part she had made up and added to the story. The part Phoebe liked the best.

"Well," she said in her best story-telling voice, "you see, rocks don't grow. Not normally. But this one does. It grows each summer. Just a little bit. So tiny that you can barely see it, but I bet if you'd snapped a picture of it a long time ago and took one now and compared 'em, you'd see a huge difference."

A small breeze fluttered through the screen. Phoebe snuggled closer to Caroline. Her toes felt strangely cold against Caroline's legs. "Who lives there?" she asked.

The crickets chirped loudly.

"I'm getting' to that part," Caroline said. "You see, this rock grows because it's got something livin' underneath it. Not worms or ants, like normal rocks. This one has fairies living under it. A whole family of fairies. And every summer new fairies are born. Fairies are only born in the summertime. So that's why the rock grows every summer—to make room for all the new fairies."

Phoebe's eyes kept drooping until they were closed.

Caroline paused. When Phoebe's breathing changed to a light snore, she rolled over on her other side and stared through the screen. It was so dark, and Peter's house was nothing more than a dot in the distance. Every star in the sky was visible.

The moon hung low over the barn. Just a little ways past it was the Growing Rock.

Caroline smiled.

The fairies were probably sound asleep too.

Chapter 4

Caroline put down the garden hoe and ran to meet Peter. Her sides ached. Salty wetness dripped off her face.

But, finally, he was there.

Peter stopped and leaned against the white fence beside the barn, holding his hat in his hands and whistling his favorite bird call, as if he had nothing in the world to worry about. He grinned and put a piece of straw in his mouth.

Caroline slapped his arm and grinned. "Bout time you got here. What took you so long?"

"Well, ain't you impatient this morning?" Peter said with the straw stuck in his front teeth. "I had to tend to all my Pap's animals first."

Of course. Peter was always working these days. He hardly ever took a break. Caroline sat on the top rail of the post fence. Even the wood felt hot against her fingertips.

"So I heard your Pa left last week."

"Yep, he did." Caroline tucked the wisps from her braid behind her ears. "Reckon he'll be back fair enough, though, seein' as I'll be carrying most of the workload at our place now."

Peter pulled the straw out and laughed. He looked around. "Blanche still actin' weird?"

"You bet. Talkin' nonstop about this fancy wedding she wants to have. I don't know how she'll ever pay for it, or who'll even want to come if she did." Blanche had broken just about every boy's heart in Ripley. A lot of girls didn't even speak to her anymore.

Peter rested one leg on the bottom rail of the fence. He shrugged. "That sister of yours is awful pretty, but awful crazy at the same time."

Caroline's heart sped up. Blanche had always been the pretty one, and no one ever criticized her. Ever since she got engaged, though, Peter seemed to agree more and more with Caroline's complaints against her.

He'd had his heart broken too.

Which was fine with Caroline. Who wanted her friends turning red every time her older sister walked in the room? She ran her fingers through her hair and adjusted Papa's hat. She hoped it made the sunburn less pink looking.

Peter started walking toward the house. Caroline had to walk fast to keep up with his long stride.

He changed the topic. "Miss Evelyn was actin' up a mighty pretty fit today."

"Really? What did she do now?"

"You remember Anna?"

Caroline nodded. Of course she remembered. She remembered everybody who'd ever come to school, even though Anna had quit coming almost a year ago.

"Well," Peter continued, "Apparently ole Evelyn accused her of pouring pop all over her windows. First thing this morning."

Caroline frowned. "First off, I doubt if Anna ever gets to treat herself to pop. Her family is far too poor, and she's always busy taking care of her eight brothers. Second off, she's not the kind to do something like that."

Peter nodded. "Funny as it would be, everyone knows better than to go stirring up trouble with ole Evelyn."

Caroline nodded and giggled. Miss Evelyn had lived in the same house on the land neighboring theirs for forty years. Her husband had died a long time ago. Her children were grown, but no one had ever seen them come for a visit. She kept odd things, like wrappers and rusty cans, and hated throwing anything away, even the most worthless items. She yelled at any child who came near her home. Charles Jackson said every time he drove by, he'd tip his hat and wave if she were outside, but she'd hold up her Bible and tell him he was of the devil for driving a car.

Peter shook an imaginary Bible in Caroline's face and bumped into her arm. "Shun the non-believer!"

Caroline stopped walking and laughed until her sides ached. That was what Miss Evelyn had yelled at them one time when she saw them walking to the pond to swim, even though they'd already told her it wasn't Sunday and there was no Sunday school class to attend that day.

"Goodness," Caroline sighed.

She shaded her eyes and glanced up, but Peter was already inside the house, getting instructions about what he needed to help with. She fanned her face. She wished it wouldn't be too pink when he came back.

But she smiled again. Having Peter around was already making the day much better.

"Race ya to the water hole," Peter shouted.

Caroline ran as fast as she could. The dirt road seemed even dustier than normal. It hadn't rained in a couple of weeks. They slowed when they passed Miss Evelyn's house.

As usual, she was on her porch, sitting in her rocking chair. But she was asleep. Her gray head leaned off to one side. A bundle of knitting dangled from her skinny, wrinkled fingers.

Miss Evelyn might have been old, but her hearing was as good as theirs. Or better.

Caroline followed Peter to the other side of the road. Their bare feet moved quickly and quietly until they were out of earshot.

Sweat poured from Caroline's forehead and burned her eyes. Her wrists and fingertips were sore and calloused from chopping cotton all morning. Thank goodness Mama told them to take a break after dinner and soak some turpentine on their hands.

When they reached the small pond, Peter jumped in.

Caroline started to join him but stopped. She didn't wear a bra yet, and, if she were to get wet, her dress would be see-through, wouldn't it? That sorta thing had never mattered before. But ever since Aunt Elsmere had arrived, things like that were a big deal.

"What are you waiting on?" Peter shouted.

Caroline looked down again. She wasn't much larger in the chest than Phoebe. It probably wouldn't make a difference to Peter. He'd never said anything before. So why did it suddenly matter to her?

Peter swam a few laps and came back to where she stood. "You getting in or what?"

Caroline dipped her toes in the water. The water felt good against her tired, dusty feet. She could at least get in up to her waist. After all, the old swimsuit she'd worn the past few years was too little. There was definitely no money for a new one, but if Aunt Elsmere or Mama complained, maybe they should've thought about it before, instead of treating her as if she were still Phoebe's age.

"I'm coming." She walked in slowly and stopped when the water hit her waist.

"Race you," Peter said.

"Nah, I—can't get my hair wet right now," she lied. The water felt cool and clean against her grimy skin.

Peter took his shirt off. As always, his stomach was the color of milk, but his arms were dark brown. It was hard not to notice how much he'd grown since the summer before. He used to be thick in the middle. Now he was tall and skinny. Dark hairs sprinkled his chest and belly button.

Caroline glanced down. It wasn't fair that he had changed so much when she hadn't changed much at all. Would she ever be pretty like Blanche? Would anyone ever look at her the way Robert looked at Blanche?

Why did she even care? Peter was just a friend. They used to play together in the front yard with nothing but their undies on. The thought made her want to wrap up in a blanket. She pulled her dress away from her body so it didn't cling to her skin and crossed her arms.

"Thank goodness Miss Evelyn didn't speak to us." Peter sat down where the water was shallow and rested his head against a rock. He wasn't paying attention to her dress.

Caroline sighed. "I know. I hope she's inside when we go back."

"Yeah, me too." Peter ran his hands through his hair. "Your Ma wants me to kill some chickens for her sometime this week."

"Oh." Quite a change in topic. "Papa mentioned something about that. Guess he didn't have time himself."

"Wish he had."

Caroline frowned. "Why? You kill pigs all the time."

"And every time, it makes me feel kinda sick to my stomach."

"Why?"

"I dunno. I don't have a problem with fish and birds and things like that. But there's something about the animals I care for every day. Guess I get kinda attached to them, especially the pigs. I hate the squeal they make when they die. It just feels wrong. Something about their eyes. Guess it's why I wanna be a doctor."

Caroline rested her knees on the muddy bottom.

Peter had to be joking. When he didn't laugh, though, it was clear he wasn't. Which made no sense because Peter had never had a problem doing a job before.

He shrugged and rested his head back in his arms. He shut his eyes. A lot had changed about Peter lately, and it wasn't just the way he looked.

The water was a nice, lukewarm. It was like being in the pond with Peter again, only this time, Caroline didn't have to worry about anyone seeing her.

Except Aunt Elsmere.

The shadow of her fat frame showed against the curtain Mama had hung up in front of the bathtub.

"I can't believe you went swimming in such a skimpy dress. You were basically naked."

Caroline scrubbed with soap one more time, even though she'd already scrubbed plenty of times. Her fingers had those wrinkles she got when she was in the water too long.

"I wear that every day."

"But not when you're soaking wet."

"I do when I swim with Phoebe."

Aunt Elsmere clicked her teeth. "Phoebe is a *girl*. And your sister. Peter is a *boy*."

"That never mattered before." Caroline rinsed the soap suds off.

"Well, it does now." Aunt Elsmere opened the curtain and tossed a towel on the edge of the tub.

So much for privacy.

Aunt Elsmere stood there, surely waiting for some saucy reply that would cause a bigger argument, but Caroline kept her mouth shut. She closed her eyes and held her breath under the water. When she put her head up for air, Aunt Elsmere had left the room. Caroline dried off and got dressed.

"Blanche," she called. "It's your turn."

Blanche came into the kitchen and grunted. She put her hands on her perfect waist. "I'll have to get fresh water."

Caroline shrugged. "Suit yourself." She walked to the front porch to let her hair dry. The old swing creaked back and forth. It never did that with Papa on it. Caroline's small frame wasn't heavy enough to stop the awful moaning sound it made.

Oil the swing. It was another thing that needed to be done.

Her stomach growled. Even though she'd already had supper, she felt tired from not eating enough throughout the day. The heat stole all her energy.

She stared into the darkening sky and hummed "His Eye is on the Sparrow." She couldn't whistle like Papa.

"Mind if I join you?" Aunt June walked up the gravel driveway and sat beside Caroline.

The creaking stopped.

"How are things going with your Pa gone?"

"It's going alright, I guess. Peter came over today."

Aunt June nodded, not noticing that Caroline had turned pink again at Peter's name.

"Yes, P. Joe told me how hard you and your friend were working today. Your Pa would be proud of you."

"Thanks." Caroline smiled.

Aunt June reached over and took the hairbrush Caroline was still holding. She brushed Caroline's long, damp hair and ran her fingers through it, twisting it in a neat French braid.

"If you take this down in the morning and only finger comb it, you'll have some pretty waves for church," she said. Her hair was red, not strawberry blonde. It was a much deeper, darker red, almost the color the flowers on the cotton plants turned right before they withered up and the fluffy cotton came through.

Neither of them spoke for a moment. Aunt June stared off in the distance, watching the lightning bugs.

"Aunt June?"

"Yes?"

"Do you ever feel kinda overwhelmed? By things changing, I mean?"

Aunt June sighed. "I think everyone does sometimes. There's an awful lot of change, and it just never stops.

"Aunt June?"

"Yes?"

"Do you ever feel like things are just never fair? Like you always have to do more than anyone else, but then you never get to do anything fun? And when you do, you get in trouble?"

Aunt June studied her for a moment. "Yeah, all the time. Growing up, it seemed like your father could do no wrong and always got his way." She shrugged. "Now we both work so much and do the best we can do. We lean on each other for help, that's for sure."

Caroline scratched a mosquito bite on her elbow. Maybe someday she and Blanche would be that way, but right now it was annoying to hear her sister constantly complain about things like dresses and clean bath water.

Aunt June crossed one leg over the other and leaned her head back.

"Your sister's one silly girl," she said, as if reading Caroline's mind. "But try not to let it get to you. You keep your head up and stay focused. Your Mama's gonna see pretty soon that you're much more grown up than she realizes."

Caroline scratched her elbow again.

Maybe Aunt June was right.

"Well, I'm gonna go speak to your Mama. She's quiet lately, and that worries me. She doesn't seem to be herself. You sit here long's you want."

"Okay." Caroline took a deep breath. Aunt June had a way of making things feel better, the way George always had. For a minute, things felt safer.

The crickets and frogs were out for the night. The lightning bugs danced around the flower bushes beside the porch railing. It was dark and quiet inside the house.

Caroline walked to the other side of the porch and stopped short. She leaned against the corner of the wall and peeked out.

Blanche and Robert held each other for the longest time, pressed against the porch railing. Robert kissed Blanche, as if he were eating her face.

Blanche ran her fingers through his hair and kissed him back, making little moaning noises and leaning toward him as close as she could. She wore a light pink romper with ruffled sleeves and a bow at the neckline. It was short enough that it showed most of her long, tanned legs. Mama had agreed for her to order it from a catalog to use as a bathing suit. But Blanche mainly wore it around the house on extra hot days.

How was it fair that Blanche could wear *that* around Robert, but Caroline couldn't get her everyday dress wet?

Blanche pressed her chest against Robert, her arms squeezing him around his neck.

Caroline's stomach tightened. What was it like to kiss someone? What did it feel like to have a boy inching his hands closer and closer to where they didn't belong? What did it *feel* like to know someone liked, or maybe even loved, you that much?

Phoebe came outside. When the door opened, Blanche and Robert quickly backed away from each other. Blanche straightened her clothes. Robert tried wiping Blanche's lipstick stains from his lips.

Caroline walked around the corner, as if she hadn't been there all along.

"Caroline," Phoebe said. "Can you come sit on the Growing Rock with us? With me and Mama and Aunt Elsmere and Aunt June?"

Blanche paused in the middle of opening the door to go inside. She grabbed Robert's hand. "That's the *dumbest* thing anyone ever heard. Don't you go around believing that, too, Phoebe. Rocks can't possibly grow. Animals and people grow."

She glanced at Caroline. "Unless your name's Caroline, and you're fourteen years old and won't grow up."

She turned around and slammed the door behind her. Robert shrugged at them through the screened door, mouthing the words, "I'm sorry."

Caroline shrugged back at him. It wasn't his fault. "Just ignore her," she told Phoebe. Maybe the story was just another thing that reminded Blanche of George.

Caroline led the way down the slight hill behind the house along a little path on the edge of the cotton field. Mama, Aunt Elsmere, and Aunt June all sat on the huge rock. Caroline helped Phoebe climb up beside Mama. Then she squeezed next to Aunt June. Aunt Elsmere and Aunt June talked and sipped lemonade, coaxing Mama to join in. Mama smiled a little now and then, but her cup sat there untouched.

Looking at the rock, it didn't seem big enough for all of them to sit, but it was. Which seemed crazy to think because even if the rock wasn't getting any larger, *they* certainly were growing themselves.

Aunt June started telling a story about when she was a teenager getting married, before the Depression and the hard times. She talked of dancing and dressing up in lovely outfits and how she met Uncle P. Joe. It seemed like a different world from the one they lived in now.

Had Aunt June been a bit like Blanche? She was definitely pretty enough to have that many boyfriends. She'd been two whole years younger than Blanche when she married, which meant only two years older than Caroline.

What would Caroline be doing in two years? She probably wouldn't be married, but would she be in school still? Where would George and Papa be?

She took a sip of Mama's sweet lemonade and leaned her head back. The stars seemed extra bright. In the distance, a tiny light shone from Peter's house. His family was lucky enough to have electricity.

Was Peter thinking about her right now, too? Did he think she was still a little girl like Mama did? After all, she was a whole year younger.

Caroline closed her eyes. She thought of swimming and what it would feel like if Peter suddenly held her the way Robert had held Blanche, if his hands traveled where Robert's had been going. Aunt Elsmere had always talked about not giving yourself to a man before you were married, but she never said what she meant by this. Caroline only learned by listening to those talks on the back porch. Was it wrong just to think about it, though?

She opened her eyes. No one was talking anymore. They all just stared at the stars and the endless darkness, trying to fight their sleepy eyelids from closing.

No, she decided. It wasn't wrong to think about things that made the hard times better. It didn't hurt to tell stories about a rock that grew either, if it meant five minutes where Phoebe could forget about being a sick, skinny, little girl. It didn't matter what Blanche said. It didn't matter what anyone thought, really.

She needed to imagine things. She needed a special rock that magically grew bigger each year. She needed to believe it for Phoebe and for Papa. And for George.

They all did.

Chapter 5

The light poured through the window of the colorful glass and sprinkled spots of rainbow here and there. Caroline concentrated on the patch of blue beside her foot, as if it mattered a great deal. In a way, it did. It mattered because it was the only thing to help her avoid Aunt Elsmere's awful glare.

It was too bad that in that moment she herself wasn't one of the fairies in the story and could hide under the Growing Rock.

"Caroline," Aunt Elsmere repeated, "Did you hear what the preacher just asked you?"

Caroline tore her eyes away from the light. Aunt Elsmere, shorter than she was, stared up and waited for an answer. She nodded toward the preacher, her double chin bouncing up and down.

"I'm sorry, what?"

Aunt Elsmere groaned. "You'll have to forgive her. She's a little distracted by that wonderful sermon."

Preacher Reveley smiled. With his red, round face, bald head, and big ears, he always reminded her of a smooth, baby pig.

"No pressure, Caroline. We're just trying to get more young people in the community to help the elderly, especially now that more of the men are away."

Caroline held her breath. Aunt Elsmere gave her the worst beady-eyed glare she possibly could. Her blood pressure was surely going up from embarrassment because she started her high-pitched giggling that meant she was about to boil over.

No pressure, whatsoever.

Just Aunt Elsmere going home and complaining about her to Mama, and Mama nagging about how a young lady needs to do her share during such hard times.

If Mama even cared enough to listen. She was so odd that morning and didn't go with them. Mama never missed a Sunday, not even when Phoebe had been her sickest.

Preacher Reveley paused at the silence. "I'm sure it would mean a great deal to Miss Evelyn if you could help. After all, you live the closest to her, and you know she doesn't get out much." He waited for an answer. "But, of course, you're very busy, I know."

Aunt Elsmere moved to lean against an empty pew and stepped on Caroline's foot.

Caroline clenched her teeth. She'd have a nice, nasty bruise in no time.

"Okay, I'll help," she finally muttered.

Preacher Reveley smiled again and moved to talk to another family. Caroline brushed some hair back over her shoulder and made her way out the door. It was hot, but even hotter in that tiny, one-room church with everyone standing close and singing and fretting over their sins. Her curls stuck to her neck.

What would Papa say about this? What was Mama going to say when she got home and told her Aunt Elsmere had done it again and forced her into volunteering to help someone who wouldn't even appreciate it?

"Little girls shouldn't ask questions."

Caroline rolled over on her back and closed *Little Women*. Grass stuck to her bare legs. She pulled her dress down.

Thank the Lord Louisa May Alcott hadn't actually believed that one. She'd been a bit like Aunt June, thinkin' that women deserved the same chances as the men. Aunt June always said that it was important to ask things whenever she wanted, even if it was questions about her monthly that Mama said weren't appropriate.

Caroline sighed. She leaned back and opened the book again. The picture of Marmee reading a letter to the four March sisters made her wish things could be the way they used to be.

She shut her eyes. If she listened closely, she could hear her family laughing and joking with one another, Mama's knitting needles gently clicking, the radio turned down real low in the background.

The memory grew more real. She began to see Thomas and Pamelia, newly engaged, playing Monopoly with Papa and George. Blanche came home from a date and joined them. Phoebe was already asleep in Aunt June's lap.

And she could imagine herself watching them with sleepy eyes from the corner of the room, huddled next to one of the kerosene lamps with her favorite book. Even though it was summertime, she'd felt chilly because she had just read the scene where Amy goes ice skating and falls through the ice. Mama wrapped a blanket around Caroline. Then she helped her upstairs and tucked both her and Phoebe into bed.

Had that only been last summer? Barely even a year ago?

Caroline opened her eyes. So much had changed since then. Aunt Elsmere had come, and George and Papa had gone.

"Caroline! Caroline!"

She brushed the grass off her legs again and stretched.

"Caroline!"

Phoebe nearly ran right over Caroline and just about lost her balance trying not to step on her.

"What is it?"

"Aunt Elsmere says you gotta help me get things ready for the Tomato Festival."

Caroline sat up. A leaf fell off her head and onto her lap. "The Tomato Festival? You mean, we're still doing *that*?"

Phoebe frowned. "Why wouldn't we? We go every year."

"Yeah, well, that was before Papa left. I bet Mama won't go."

"Mama said you'd take me."

Caroline's face grew hot. Why did Mama think she could promise Phoebe things from other people? What gave her the right?

"She did, did she?"

Phoebe followed her gaze toward the house. "You'll take me, won't you?"

"I need to go inside for a minute. I'm really hot."

Phoebe flopped down in Caroline's spot. She couldn't read, but she liked to look at the pictures and pretend she could.

Mama was sitting at the kitchen table, staring out the window. She didn't even look up when Caroline entered.

"Mama?"

Mama jumped in surprise. Her arm knocked over a glass of water.

"Good gravy, you scared me, Caroline! Sneakin' up like that." She stood up and wiped the table with a dry rag.

"Mama, it's important. Did you tell Phoebe I'd take her to that blasted tomato thing again?"

Mama continued wiping the table, as if she hadn't heard a word. Maybe she hadn't. She hated when the girls said "blasted."

"Mama, did you hear me?"

Mama sat down again. She rubbed her eyes. "Sorry, honey, I'm just tired."

Caroline took a deep breath. "Well, I wanted you to know that I don't think I'm taking Phoebe to that festival. I don't want to go this year cause it's the same day as the Bisbee Show."

Mama finally looked at her. Her eyes seemed darker than normal underneath.

"You don't have money for that. The Tomato Festival is free. It's a Ripley tradition. You're going to that instead."

Why did Mama have to be so negative?

"But I don't *want* to go to the festival. I don't care about tomatoes. I don't even *like* tomatoes."

Mama turned and looked out the window again.

Caroline's voice grew louder. She moved closer to the table. "I don't *want* to go. Why can't *you* take Phoebe? Why can't you do *anything*?"

Mama's shoulders shook. A few tears spilled down her cheeks, and before Caroline knew it, Mama was sobbing. Mama, who she'd only seen cry one time before, when Phoebe had almost died.

Caroline's breath caught in her throat. She moved closer to lay her hand on Mama's shoulder. "Mama, I—"

"What's your problem?" Blanche stormed in the room. "Why do you always have to be such a selfish pig and make things worse? Can't you see she's upset?"

"I'm sorry. I didn't—"

Blanche slapped her hand. "You didn't think, did you? Well, maybe you should think more often."

Caroline took a step back. Tears burned the backs of her eyes.

Mama sobbed even more.

Aunt Elsmere's heavy frame thumped down the stairs. A moment later she was in there too. "What's going on?" her voice boomed.

"Caroline was causing trouble again," Blanche said, rubbing Mama's shoulder where Caroline's hand had been.

"She wasn't the only one." Aunt Elsmere glared at Blanche. "I'm ashamed of you two. Both acting so selfish. I'm not so sure you need to go to The Bisbee Show either. Shouldn't you and Robert be saving money?"

Blanche's face was red. She looked down at the floor. It was the first time since Aunt Elsmere moved in that she'd ever complained about Blanche.

Aunt Elsmere turned toward Caroline. "And as for you, it's a good thing you're volunteering for the church. It'll keep you outta trouble.

"Now get out of here, both of you."

Blanche stormed up the stairs. Caroline ran back outside. She ran past Phoebe and the big oak tree, past the rose bushes and the vegetable garden. She stopped when she got to the Growing Rock and sat down. It felt warm beneath her bare feet, but it didn't matter.

If it hadn't been a Sunday, goodness knows what punishment Aunt Elsmere would've given them.

Caroline rubbed her hand, still tingling from where Blanche had slapped it.

Before Caroline had time to get used to the idea, it was already Wednesday. Time to go work for Miss Evelyn and do whatever she needed done.

She hadn't even seen Peter since Sunday. Now, as she sat in that tiny, sweltering hot kitchen by herself, her arms covered up to her elbows with flour from baking loaves of bread, it was hard not to wonder if she'd ever get to leave. Would Peter have already come and gone by the time she returned home? He was supposed to come over to help that afternoon.

Miss Evelyn's big, gold clock told her that time was passing very slowly. Preacher Reveley had walked her over a half hour ago. He wanted to "properly" introduce her to Miss Evelyn. What a joke that was. Everyone in Ripley knew everyone. And everyone knew it.

But she hadn't complained. Nothin' was more awkward than going to someone's home alone when that person had yelled at you a dozen times every week every summer for cutting through her yard. Or messing up her flowers trying to find a baseball that was unlucky enough to fall that close to her house.

Mama always said not to play ball in that field between their home and Miss Evelyn's. But George had anyway. So everyone else did, too. Though Caroline probably wouldn't this summer, or at least as long as Aunt Elsmere was around.

Caroline washed her hands in the kitchen sink. Miss Evelyn was lucky to have electricity and running water in her home. It felt cleaner and colder than the well water ever did. She put both of her arms underneath the faucet and washed the flour off. It was too bad she couldn't put her face beneath it, too. It was kind of like swimming the other day with Peter. And that made Aunt Elsmere's face with her beady eyes and lips that always smirked come to mind.

Aunt Elsmere was the one who should have been in that kitchen, not Caroline. After all, she was the one who wanted to help so much. The two ladies would probably become friends—Aunt Elsmere sitting on that front porch, fanning herself with one of those big fans Miss Evelyn liked to use, both of them fussing and moaning about anyone having fun or doing something with their lives besides complain.

Something tapped the wooden floor. Miss Evelyn had come back inside and stood there stomping her tiny foot. She looked like a chicken with that crazy gray, white hair all ruffled like a bunch of feathers.

"I see you have the bread all in the oven," she said.

"Yes, ma'am." Caroline's face felt bright red. That kitchen had to be hotter than it was outside.

Miss Evelyn hesitated. Maybe she'd let her go home. Caroline crossed her fingers.

"I have another project for you to do," she said instead. Miss Evelyn walked out the back door, and Caroline followed, drying her hands on her dress.

They went inside a little shed by the side of the house. Stacks of wooden vegetable crates and old gardening tools made it hard to walk very far inside it, and Caroline stopped to let her eyes adjust to the dim lighting. Several large jars of slimy green juice and brownish green clumps that looked like cow manure sat on one of the shelves in front of her.

Miss Evelyn smiled at Caroline's frown. Her yellowing teeth were chipped in the front.

"Those are my mama's special sweet pickles."

Bile rose up Caroline's throat. Her *mother's* pickles? Miss Evelyn had to be near seventy or eighty years old, which meant those pickles might've been just as old or older. They could've been a hundred.

That morning's breakfast of biscuits and onion started leaving a taste in her mouth. She swallowed hard so she wouldn't lose those biscuits in front of Miss Evelyn.

Miss Evelyn watched closely.

"You look flushed," she said. She handed Caroline a basket of clothespins. "Go hang my laundry up, then come back and see me."

Caroline nodded and took the clothespins. When she was around the corner of the house and Miss Evelyn couldn't see her, she threw up all big and nasty. Right behind one of those flower bushes that George had trampled so many times.

If two hours felt like four, then four hours felt like eight. It seemed as if she'd never leave. Like the whole thing was some awful trick, some wicked plan where she'd stay there forever and work for Miss Evelyn and the day would never end, the sun never set.

She hoped Peter would wait on her so she could at least tell him about how horrible it all was and they could get a good laugh out of it.

Caroline handed Miss Evelyn the basket of clean clothes.

"The wet ones are all hanging to dry."

Miss Evelyn acted as if she hadn't heard. She handed her some gardening gloves and a basket. "Go pull some fresh tomatoes," she said.

Just the word "tomatoes" made Caroline gag again. What was it with everyone and those blasted tomatoes? What was wrong with Ripley? Could they not think of anything more exciting than tomatoes? If they were going to have a festival for food, couldn't it be for something that was at least tasty? Like grapes or apples?

Still, picking tomatoes was probably better than being in that steaming kitchen. And definitely better than being near that shed with those horrible pickles.

The tomato patch was just behind the house, so she took the basket and got to work. She went to the very back of the small garden and worked her way toward the house so she wouldn't have to be near Miss Evelyn for a while.

It was odd that tomatoes were the only thing Miss Evelyn had left on the farm. No animals, no cotton, no other fruits or vegetables.

All that land, but just a small garden of those blasted tomatoes.

It was even stranger that she had some of the best tomatoes around. Not that Caroline ever tried them, but everyone talked about how perfect they were. Just by looking at them, it was easy to see they were much better than the ones at home. Large and plump, no mushy spots.

Caroline hummed that Shirley Temple song about the "Good Ship Lollipop." The sky had grown overcast, so at least her scalp wouldn't get any more sunburned than it already was.

She worked as quickly as she could. She was somewhere in the middle of the garden and had just reached the part for the fourth time about landing on a chocolate bar when an old, scrawny squirrel came up and started tearing off a small tomato.

She always had to shoo off animals back home, but what was the point in bothering with this one? It was just one tiny tomato, and how many did one old lady need anyhow? It was kind of nice having someone else there in that garden. Even if it was just a squirrel.

It didn't see her at first, but when it did, it twitched and looked around, as if it wondered if she was dangerous.

Caroline giggled. "I won't do nothin' to hurt you."

She crouched down on her knees and took one of the smallest tomatoes out of the big basket and placed it a few feet away.

It inched its way toward her, looking unsure and scared, its tiny black eyes darting to the left and right.

"Come on, I'm not mean. I promise."

The next thing that happened, happened so fast.

Out of nowhere, a gunshot popped. Caroline fell backwards, knocking over the basket. Her body trembled. She looked all around. Miss Evelyn stood a little ways behind her with a small rifle dangling at her side.

"People ask why my tomatoes are the best. Now ya know." She twirled the gun back and forth. "I don't let nothin' bother em. Don't matter what it is. I do what I gotta do."

She moved closer and tried handing her the gun.

Caroline shook her head and turned away toward the squirrel.

It still stared back at her, its eyes unmoving. A small dribble of red liquid oozed at its side from underneath its belly.

It was so warm, and the sun was coming out from behind the clouds again. Caroline's head ached. Was Miss Evelyn crazier than they'd always said? Was that even possible?

Miss Evelyn walked back inside her house with the basket.

Go home. Over and over these two words rang through Caroline's mind, but her legs felt as if they'd never be able to move again. She was rooted to the ground like one of those wired tomato cages.

That squirrel stared at her. Had it only been moments before that she was playing with it?

She'd killed a few animals before, when she'd had to. Twisted chickens' throats and never given much thought to it. It was just part of living on a farm.

But Papa had always said you didn't kill anything unless it was for a reason and you needed it. And then you didn't waste it. You didn't kill something just because.

It was something about those tiny eyes. Maybe that was what Peter meant when he said he couldn't kill a cow and not feel bad.

The tears started coming. Vomit seeped up her throat again, and she got a mouthful of liquid that tasted like onions. The sudden thought of those pickles almost made her cough up another, but she swallowed. Her throat burned and felt raw from the acid taste.

She wiped her mouth on the hem of her dress and tried not to look at the squirrel.

Go home. Her legs got their feeling back, and she stood up. When it seemed as if Miss Evelyn wasn't looking, that's exactly what she did.

Caroline ran home.

And there was no way she'd be coming back next Wednesday.

"How'd it go?" Peter asked, the corners of his lips curling up. He'd already helped Phoebe gather all the best tomatoes in their garden. He knew how much Caroline hated them.

Caroline groaned. "Just glad it's over."

"Was she mean?" Phoebe asked.

Caroline shrugged. "Not as bad as I thought," she lied. "Just kinda sat there and watched what I did. She had some gross old pickles that looked like manure."

Peter laughed.

No point in telling them about the squirrel. Phoebe cried when anything was the slightest bit sad.

The back door opened. Aunt Elsmere poked her head outside.

"Caroline, there you are. I was just wondering when you'd be back. While Peter's helping your mother by working in the fields, I need you to help me and Blanche fix the pies for the festival."

Nasty. Make those nasty tomato pies that everyone else loved in that crammed, steaming hot kitchen, instead of working with Peter? It was just as bad as going back to Miss Evelyn's house for the rest of the day.

Aunt Elsmere glanced at Peter. So that was it. She was still mad about them going swimming the other day and didn't want them around each other.

Aunt June came around the side of the porch all of a sudden. Her red hair was puffing in all directions from the heat of the kitchen. She wiped her hands on her apron.

"There you are, Caroline. I was just gonna ask if you could help me make the sauce for the pies. Blanche is slicing up the tomatoes." She turned to Peter. "And, hello, Peter. It's so good to see you, and thank you again for helping us womenfolk. Would you like to stay for supper?"

Caroline smiled. Aunt June always knew how to make things better.

Chapter 6

Phoebe bounced up and down with her tomato basket. She was lucky she wasn't twelve yet. She was too young to be entered for a chance to be Tomato Queen, which meant she didn't have to wear red, though she wore it anyhow.

Everyone always thought you had to wear red in order to win. But how boring was that?

Well, obviously not boring to Blanche. After all the fuss about not having anything to wear, there she was hogging the mirror and wearing her signature red dress and matching red lipstick. Aunt Elsmere had twisted part of her hair up in an elaborate bun, the rest hanging in big curls.

"I wonder who will win the crown this year," Blanche smirked. She sucked her stomach in and tightened the sash on her dress more. Though she was too old to enter the Tomato Pageant, in many ways, she would still be the winner.

Caroline sat on the edge of the bed and tucked her legs underneath her. She'd sit there as long as she could, up until the minute they had to walk out the door, before she'd put her own awful red dress on.

Mama poked her head inside. "My, how lovely my girls look." She glanced at the lilac dress Blanche had thrown aside on the bed. The dress she'd added lace to and mended not long after Papa left. Her jaw tightened.

Her eyes met Caroline's. "If your sister doesn't want to wear this, you should."

"Really? You mean it?"

"But I entered her in the contest," Aunt Elsmere interrupted. "She must wear red."

Mama looked tiredly from the dress to Caroline and back again. "Caroline's doing me a favor by going with Phoebe tonight. If this dress fits, there's no reason why she can't put it to use." She glanced at Caroline again. "That red ain't going well with her complexion."

Either Mama felt bad about making her go, or she knew she wouldn't ever stand a chance of winning anyway. Or maybe she was mad she wasted time fixing a dress Blanche wasn't going to wear. It didn't matter, though. Anything was better than that red.

Mama and Aunt Elsmere both left the room with Phoebe trailing behind them. They took the kerosene lamp, so Blanche lit two candles.

Caroline jumped up and tossed the red dress aside. The lilac one fell over her head easily. It was soft and airy, not itchy under the arms like the red one.

"Blanche, help me tie the bow."

Blanche sighed. "Oh, all right." She set her lipstick on the dresser and turned around. She glanced up and down. "Not bad. I bet you'll get some curves soon."

"Really?" Caroline turned to face the mirror. Blanche had tied the bow real tight, only Caroline just looked thin and straight, not like the hour glass at school, the way Blanche did. The dress was also a little looser at the top than it had been on Blanche. But maybe Blanche was right. Maybe she was growing and didn't know it. Like the Growing Rock. At least she didn't look like a tomato now; she just had a soft glow in her cheeks.

"Oh, if only you had a little brassiere, it would do wonders."

"Yeah, but Aunt Elsmere said that's a waste of money, since there's nothin' there yet."

Blanche sighed and rolled two pairs of socks and put them in the top of Caroline's dress.

Caroline's face turned pink. "Blanche, how old were you when—you know—became a woman?"

Blanche looked away and turned to her makeup instead. "Has Mama talked to you about all that?"

"Well, no. But I hear you all sayin' things when you think I'm not listenin'. And other girls at school who have their monthly already talk about it sometimes."

"Mama really needs to be the one to explain it to you, though." Blanche sighed. "But I was twelve."

Of course Blanche had been younger. She got to do everything early.

"How old were you when you got your first kiss?"

"Hmmm. I think I was thirteen."

Again, younger.

"Well—what do you do when someone kisses you? I mean, how do you know what to do with your lips?"

Blanche laughed. "Oh, you'll know what to do. It's not that big of a deal. Just kiss him back."

Caroline groaned on the inside. If anyone ever kissed her.

"Now don't you be so down. I'm betting your time's coming. You'll be telling me one of these days soon that Peter kissed you."

Caroline adjusted the top of her dress. Now her face probably looked like a tomato again.

It wasn't completely dark outside yet, but headlights shone against the house for a second. Through the openings in the curtain she could see Robert and someone else getting out of a car.

"What's Charles Jackson doing here?" Caroline backed away from the window so that no one would see her looking out.

"He's not the only one with a car. It's Robert's friend who's staying for the summer."

Blanche looked in the mirror one last time, pursing her red lips together, her face flushed. She blew out the candle she'd been using. "Have fun, Caroline. I'll see you later."

Caroline blew the other candle out and lay in the semi-darkness until Phoebe knocked on the door three times saying they'd already missed the first hour of the festival, and if they didn't hurry they'd miss the crowning for that year's queen. Caroline pulled the socks out of her dress and stuffed them in a dresser drawer. It wouldn't be any good if they fell out on the dance floor.

"Coming," she said, forcing her voice to sound somewhat excited.

Too bad she didn't have George this year.

"Well, aren't you two just as pretty as ever?" Aunt June said coming from behind the booth she'd set up. "Us Neal girls know how to throw the boys for a loop, don't we?"

Phoebe pulled Caroline's arm. "Can I go sit with Annie and Debra Jean, please? We wanna sit on the front row and see the queen!"

"Okay, okay." Just meet me right here when you're done, okay?" Caroline said. Aunt Elsmere had entered her in the contest, but she wasn't even going up to the small platform where all the other girls were lined up.

Phoebe ran to the front, her pigtails flopping behind her. Already, there were rows of tables set up for the tomato tastings, pie contests, and all the other nasty things people kept coming up with. It was pretty with everything lit up with lanterns and candles, but tonight was just the boring speech they heard year after year about how the festival began, how it brought the community together, and then the crowning of the queen ceremony. They'd already missed some of the smaller contests, thank goodness.

Caroline sighed. "Want me to help you set anything up?"

"Nah," Aunt June said. "You run off and have fun."

At Caroline's blank look, Aunt June laughed. "Well, I know you don't wanna be here.

Your Mama told me that. I was the one who told her she needed to make you come anyway."

"What? How could you?"

"Cause I ain't as dumb as people seem to think. Marlene and Elsmere can say all they want to, but I don't give a hoot." She glanced sideways at Caroline. "Don't tell them I said that either. "Point is, the tomato festival lasts two days, and that Bisbee Show is *only* tonight."

"Yeah, so?"

"So, you do me a favor and run off and have fun. I'll keep an eye on Phoebe for you, if you promise you'll spend the day with her tomorrow and not make a fuss about it. Your Mama worries me lately. She don't need you girls actin' up at home."

Caroline opened her mouth, but Aunt June opened her purse first. "Here's some money. Now go enjoy yourself."

"Aunt June, you don't have to do this. That's a lot of money, and a dollar is too much anyhow."

"Not if you invite a friend to go. That Peter's a sweet kid. He's helping his parents with things too and looked earlier like he was stuck with his little sisters. Why don't you ask him?"

Caroline's heart sped up. The crowds were growing larger by the minute, and the air smelled as if they were inside one giant tomato. Candles were now lit all around the platform so people could see where the queen would stand.

If she didn't leave soon, she'd be trapped there.

"Please take it." Aunt June held out the dollar bill. As Caroline reached over to take it, Aunt June pulled her hand back for a second. "Just bring me back something good and sweet, okay? These tomato pies are disgusting."

Caroline hugged Aunt June. "Thanks so much," she whispered into her curly hair.

Then she made her way through the mob of people to find Peter.

Bing Crosby's voice crooned from the record player on the stage. The couples were dancing slowly, the band resting, everyone tired from that last Duke Ellington song.

"This song's so corny," Peter said, taking a sip of lemonade. "Who cares about how great this Leilani person is? It's just the same thing again and again. Some guy talking about how she's his heaven. If she's so wonderful, why does he have to keep telling her that?"

"I think it's sweet. Maybe that's why it's called '*Sweet Leilani*'." Caroline shrugged, finishing her second bottle of Coca Cola. She probably sounded irritated, but she couldn't help it. She *was* irritated. Irritated and annoyed because no matter how many hints she'd dropped, Peter still didn't seem to get the message that she wanted to dance.

Her feet tapped underneath the table. Her whole body just about trembled with the desire to dance.

Blanche sat across the tent, taking a break from all the dancing she'd done. By now, her feet were probably blistered from so much dancing. She was talking to some fellow with dark hair and a perfectly starched suit who looked several years older than she was. He must have been the person who drove them all there. Blanche's friend, Betty, and Robert both sat there looking sulky.

Blanche had danced all night. Yet only once or so with Robert. Clearly, Caroline wasn't the only person having trouble trying to get someone else to take a hint.

Blanche didn't care, though. She ignored Robert's frustrated looks and kept laughing and talking, her face flushed, looking prettier than ever.

And flirting with Betty's date.

Her red dress stood out sharply against the white tent. Every man there couldn't help but steal a glance her way every now and then.

Caroline sighed. All she'd wanted for weeks was to go to that Bisbee Show, and now that she was there, nothing sounded better than going home. She just wasn't pretty like Blanche. She was thin—the plainest kind of thin—not the curvy kind. Not the Blanche kind. Her dress was better than that awful red one she'd worn earlier, but now she wished she'd given the socks a chance. Maybe she wouldn't have had a problem, since she wasn't dancing and moving a lot anyway.

It was just like last year. Except now she was more alone than ever. It made her so mad, that before she thought twice, she stood up.

"Where are you going?" Peter asked.

"I came here to dance, so I'm gonna dance," Caroline said. She downed the last swig of Coca-Cola and slammed the bottle on the table.

Robert wasn't surprised when she walked up. "Well, if your sister isn't going to give a fellow a fair chance, I might as well dance with you, kiddo." He lightly took one of her hands in his.

They danced quickly, and Robert didn't say much. Caroline stared at his shoulders and tried not to look at his face, which she could see up this close hadn't been shaved in a few days.

"You okay, kiddo?"

"Yes," she said. She couldn't tell him the truth. That it was her first dance at the Bisbee Show, and she hadn't wanted it to be with her sister's fiancé.

Robert's eyes had stopped looking over in Blanche's direction and now focused on her. The music had stopped. His eyes were brown, not blue like George's, but the look he gave her, so full of concern, reminded her of George. She let go of his arm.

"I'll be okay," she said. "What about you?"

"Oh, I'm fine. You go dance now with that friend of yours." He nodded toward Peter.

"I don't think he's that interested."

"I saw him watching us dance. He's interested."

"Really? You think so?"

"I know so. You go get him to dance, and I'll go try to pull Blanche away from all these other fellas."

"Robert?"

"Yeah?"

"Thank you." Caroline stood on her tiptoes and kissed Robert on the cheek, the way she had many times with George. The stubble on his face tickled. His breath smelled like the whiskey George used to sometimes sneak into the house.

"You're welcome, kiddo." Robert grinned.

"Let's go do something else," Caroline said as soon as she walked up to Peter. Maybe if Peter would get the hint that if they weren't going to dance, she didn't want to stay that much longer then he would ask her.

But, of course, he didn't understand that either.

"Okay," he said, sitting up straighter. "Wanna go ride the Ferris wheel?"

Caroline hesitated. That huge round wheel spun round and round with all them bright lights. George had wanted to ride it so badly last year, but not even he knew how to sneak on without being caught.

Peter grinned and shrugged his shoulders. "You want to?"

The extra change was still in her pocket. They didn't have to sneak on now. How could she say no? She'd have to ride. At least once, for George. That way there'd be something more exciting than the story at Miss Evelyn's house to tell him when he returned.

"Sure," Caroline said. "Why not?"

Peter didn't let her pay for it. He had exactly the right amount of change, and he paid before she could say anything. They waited in line for ten minutes, and by the time they finally got on, it was only another moment before they slowly started to lift off of the ground. Maybe it was from all the soda in her anxious stomach, or maybe it was because she'd never been so high up before, but she started feeling dizzy. She clenched her teeth and held onto the railing until her knuckles turned white.

Peter moved, and the bar for their feet shook. The whole seat swung back and forth. It kept going higher and higher as more people got on.

Caroline wasn't scared of things the way Phoebe was. So she probably wouldn't be afraid of heights. Maybe she just wouldn't allow herself to be. And then she looked down.

There were lots of lights at all the food booths. The musicians played a Benny Goodman song, and if she listened real close, she could still hear people's feet tapping against the wooden floor in the dance tent, or girls giggling as they got lifted off the ground.

In the distance was the fence George had helped her climb over the year before. And beyond that, darkness. Somewhere in that darkness, somewhere in the world, was George. And Papa.

Caroline's eyes got a little wet thinking about it all, and that just made things worse. No one wanted to be around a baby. The wheel started moving faster when all the seats were filled. A tear dribbled down Caroline's cheek, and she brushed it away.

That was when Peter put his hand on top of hers. "Hey, it's okay. Nothing to worry about."

His hand felt good and warm against her cold one. A tingle went through her whole body.

"It's okay," Peter said again.

He smiled. The lights around them made rainbow spots on his face.

How like a boy to say so. Of course it wasn't okay. Caroline had waited for years to have a boy hold her hand, and here it was, happening, and she hadn't been prepared.

But it still felt so good. It would've been even better if he could've gotten closer. Or if she could lean herself up against him. But, of course, she didn't.

"Just don't let go, okay?" Caroline whispered.

He held her hand tighter. "I won't. Promise."

That warm, tingly feeling rushed through her again, almost like a shiver, only it wasn't cold.

Peter squeezed her fingers between his. What did that mean? What was she supposed to do next? No one had ever told her how to hold a boy's hand. Was she doing it the right way? All those times she'd listened in on the back porch, and there wasn't one single time anyone talked about how to hold a hand the right away.

Maybe there was no right or wrong way. Maybe all she had to do was hold his hand back.

But it couldn't possibly be the same thing as holding Mama or Papa's hand, or Phoebe's. Surely there was a better way to do it.

Peter rubbed the top of her hand with his free hand, as if trying to warm it. It was easy to feel every callous on his skin.

"Caroline, are you okay?" he asked.

His face was so close, she could count all three of the freckles on the top of his nose. Was he going to kiss her?

Caroline closed her eyes for a second. At least that much everyone knew. You were supposed to shut your eyes whenever a boy kissed you. Blanche had said that one loads of times.

But when she looked back up, he'd turned away and was gazing up at the sky. Before she could stop herself, she leaned her head against his shoulder. His arms were large and strong, not at all like they'd been the last couple of years, when he was softer and rounder, not strong enough to hold her that long when she'd climbed on his shoulders for a game of chicken at the pond. He smelled good and sweet. He must have taken some of his Pa's cologne.

The moon was full and clear, and the stars were bright, but not as bright as normal with all the extra light from the show.

The ride stopped. Suddenly they were at the ground again. The man pulled the handle bar away so they could get out.

Peter let go of her hand, looking a little embarrassed. Her hand was cold and empty again.

It was too bad they had to get off and couldn't just keep going and going, round and round, and higher and higher.

It was too bad he couldn't keep holding her hand.

After all, she'd forgotten about the heights.

When they got back to the Tomato Festival, most people had already left. Aunt June sat alone at her booth.

"I'm so sorry, Caroline. Phoebe starting getting a little feverish—maybe it was too much excitement, I don't know—but I took her on home a short while ago. Your Mama was real worried about her, but I think she'll be okay."

"Oh, no. I sure hope so." Caroline gulped. "Did Mama ask about me?"

Aunt June smiled when Peter handed her a bag of caramel popcorn. "Why, thank you, sugar. Awfully kind of y'all to remember." She untied the bag and took a piece from the top. She didn't look Caroline in the eye. "She and Elsmere weren't too happy you weren't here with us. But I wouldn't worry too much. It was my fault, after all."

"No, it wasn't."

Aunt June ate another piece of popcorn. She held the bag out, offering some to Peter. "Well, I gave you the money for it."

"But I didn't have to accept it."

Aunt June shrugged. "Suit yourself. Just know that I already told 'em what happened." She put a cover over her table and set the last of the leftover pies in her basket. "They're not too gung-ho with me about the whole thing, but that's just how it is. Now, if Phoebe's well enough to come tomorrow, you be here bright and early for the tomato flapjack contest."

Caroline groaned. How could anyone eat that for breakfast? Peter coughed, choking on his popcorn, as if he was trying to hold back a laugh.

Aunt June patted Peter on the back. "I'm glad you two got to have some fun. Y'all can tell me all about it in the morning."

Peter beamed. "Yes'm. I'll see you then." He turned to Caroline and paused. "Good night, Caroline."

Peter left with his parents, and Aunt June and Uncle P. Joe walked home in silence with Caroline.

It wasn't like the two of them to be so quiet. Was Mama madder than Aunt June was letting on? What was Aunt Elsmere going to say? Every step they took on that piece of road—farther and farther away from those lights and music— brought her closer to some sort of punishment, surely. Aunt Elsmere wouldn't let this go.

It's all your fault. Phoebe's sick. It's all your fault, the gravel seemed to say as Caroline's feet, now numb from walking so much in her outgrown Sunday shoes, shuffled along.

They reached the front door. All the windows in the front of the house were open just like normal. But it didn't look as if any candles were lit.

"See you tomorrow," Aunt June said, giving her arm a small squeeze.

"Good night. And thanks for everything." Caroline hugged her.

"'Night," Uncle P. Joe said, his hands buried in his pockets.

When she got inside, no one was in sight. They must've all been in bed already.

Phoebe was probably sleeping in Mama's room because the bedroom was empty when she got there. Caroline changed clothes and jumped in the bed. Blanche would be home soon. She rolled on her side to stare out the window and up at the moon again. She held her right hand in between the fingers of her left hand, trying to reimagine what it had felt like when Peter had held it.

But, of course, it didn't feel the same at all. Caroline brushed her hand across her mouth.

Once, a long time ago, Peter had kissed her smack on the lips.

They were sitting on the porch like they did every summer day. No one else was around, except Mama and Papa walking up the driveway. They didn't see them sitting there on the porch. Papa bent down and kissed Mama. She giggled, and then he picked her up as if she was as light as one of the kids, spinning her around in circles.

Caroline didn't feel embarrassed about things like that. She loved it when Mama and Papa acted that way. It was so romantic.

"Have you ever kissed a girl?"

Peter looked at her as if she was crazy. "Well, no." He sat there, picking at a scab on his hand. "Have you ever kissed a boy?"

"Of course not. I'm only nine."

He nodded. "I'm only ten."

"Well, ten is double digits. You should probably kiss someone soon."

They sat there, neither one saying anything.

"Blanche says it's like magic." Caroline glanced sideways at him. "I want to know what it's like, don't you?"

Peter nodded again.

"Well, then, why don't you kiss me? Then we can both see what it's like?"

Peter shrugged and nodded a third time. He leaned over, and his lips just barely touched hers.

"I didn't feel anything," he said, looking relieved.

"Me neither. That wasn't so great, I guess. I don't see what all the fuss is."

It had happened fast, so fast they never spoke of it again afterwards.

Now, five years later, Caroline smiled in the darkness. Peter had always been her best friend.

Was it strange, then, that she wanted to hold his hand again? Was he just trying to be nice? After all, they'd grown up doing everything together.

What was it he'd wanted to say when they'd said goodbye, but couldn't because Aunt June was standing there? He'd hesitated. Was he going to kiss her? Was he going to tell her he only wanted to be friends? He was a whole year older, after all. Maybe there was someone else in his grade he liked better. A year made a big difference sometimes.

But, no matter what he had meant by it all, he *had* paid for her ticket and held her hand.

Caroline shivered. Whatever it was, the feeling she'd had earlier definitely wasn't one she'd felt before.

Nearly another hour passed before Blanche arrived. Caroline had begun to doze off when the door opened and Blanche stumbled over Caroline's shoes.

"Damn it," Blanche muttered.

Caroline sat up and lit the candle beside the bed. "It's okay. I'm still up."

Blanche smiled. "Good. I'm not sleepy yet, even though it's so late. Is Mama asleep yet?"

"I guess, and Phoebe's with her cause she felt sick."

"Oh, no." Blanche peeled off her dress and pulled a nightgown over her head. "Well, at least they don't know I'm an hour past curfew."

"I thought your curfew was at ten."

"It is. I just got to stay out extra tonight, but I'm still late."

Blanche crawled into bed underneath the covers. With the window up, it was kind of chilly. The wind blew as if it was going to rain.

"So how was your night?"

Caroline propped up on her side to face Blanche. "Well, I was home just a little bit ago.

But it was good. I rode the Ferris wheel. What about you?"

"It was so good." Blanche sighed and pulled the sheets over her chest. "He's really something, Caroline."

They were silent for a minute. It started sprinkling, and Caroline got up to shut the window. She blew the candle out.

"Blanche, what's it like to be in love?"

Blanche propped her head on her hand. "It's amazing. I don't even know how else to describe it. And all those boys I've dated in the past—they were just dates. I've never felt this way until now. It happened so fast."

Caroline put her cold feet against Blanche's legs and made her jump. Blanche hit her with a pillow. They laughed until Aunt Elsmere knocked on the door and said to be quiet.

"Well, that's good, Blanche," Caroline whispered. "You looked very pretty tonight."

"Thanks. You did too."

Caroline was almost asleep when Blanche sighed and said, "He's just such a gentleman. And what a car."

"Robert doesn't have a car," Caroline murmured, her face now turned toward the wall, her eyes closed. The rain started to fall much faster, hitting the roof with a steady beat.

Blanche muttered something that sounded an awful lot like, "I'm not talking about Robert."

Chapter 7

Caroline never thought she'd miss out on anything by skipping a day of the Tomato Festival, but seeing Phoebe in bed, pale and feverish, was enough to make anyone feel guilty about complaining so much.

"Are you okay?" Caroline placed another wet rag on Phoebe's forehead. It still felt hot and flushed. Yet Phoebe had a sheet over her, as if the sweltering bedroom were chilly.

Phoebe moaned and rolled over. The featherbed mattress looked lumpy on the side Mama never slept on. The side that was Papa's. Now it was uneven and made Phoebe's small frame look even smaller.

Caroline tried spreading the lumps out.

Oh, why had she fussed about going last night? Maybe if she had stayed with Phoebe and Aunt June like she was supposed to, none of this would've happened. Maybe Phoebe wouldn't be sick again.

Aunt Elsmere entered with a bowl of soup and a glass of water on a tray. "Gonna try to get her to eat something if she feels up to it," she whispered.

Caroline nodded. If Phoebe got real sick again, she didn't have any more weight to lose.

Aunt Elsmere brushed Phoebe's tangled hair from her face and helped her sit up. "Here," she said, holding the spoon up to Phoebe's white face, "Try this like a good girl. It will give you strength."

Phoebe swallowed maybe a spoonful or two. "My tummy's full."

Aunt Elsmere took a big breath. Her chest stuck out for a second, like it did when she was angry and about to yell. She exhaled sharply instead. Her short bangs blew away from her forehead for a second. She turned on Caroline.

"Take this tray downstairs. Then I guess make yourself useful since you're not going to that Tomato Festival now."

The way she said it sounded mad. Mad and frustrated. Aunt Elsmere must've been angry not only because Caroline hadn't won, or even tried to win the Tomato Queen pageant, but she had skipped out last night. With a boy. The same boy she'd been swimming with.

"Yes, ma'am." Caroline put the tray downstairs and started washing the pile of dishes in the tin basin under the kitchen window.

But she only washed a few plates before Mama and Blanche walked in.

Blanche wore a huge smile on her face. "Caroline, Thomas and Pamelia are havin' a baby! Guess that's why she's been throwing up so much lately."

"Blanche!" Mama snapped. Her face turned pink. "Pamelia is expecting. That's why we haven't seen her in a while."

Caroline's mind raced. A baby! How wonderful that would be. How could Mama possibly not be more excited?

"Expecting." That's what Mama and Aunt Elsmere said when anyone had a baby. That's what they'd always said when Caroline was younger and asked about a growing belly. As if someone were expecting a dinner guest. Then all of a sudden, there'd be a baby around. She'd been supposed to help take care of babies in the past, without even knowing how'd they'd gotten there.

Caroline had known better than to ask questions. She'd learned things by listening in long enough to those talks on the back porch. But now a new thought worried her. Would Papa be back in time for its birth? To see his first grandchild?

"Now," Mama held up an envelope. "We went by the post office on our way back. Got something that'll make Phoebe feel better."

"A letter!" Caroline reached out her wet hand to grab it. "Is it from George?"

Mama pulled back so Caroline couldn't reach it. At the mention of George's name, Mama's face turned sad looking, as if she'd just tasted a sour onion.

"No, stupid," Blanche said, rolling her eyes. "How many times do we have to tell you?"

"Girls, don't argue, please." Mama's voice took on a fake cheerfulness. "It's from your father."

The girls crowded around Mama's bed listening to Mama read Papa's letter. Phoebe sat propped up on pillows. A plate with untouched cookies rested at her fingertips. Aunt Elsmere was determined to get Phoebe to fatten up some. But it looked as if it was going to be a tough battle to win.

"To all *my lovely 'Little Women*,'" Mama began. She glanced at Caroline.

Caroline grinned. Papa had written that just for her.

"*I hope y'all are all doing well, and I miss you bunches. Guess by the time this reaches you, you'll have started the Tomato Festival. Eat lots of June's pies for me, especially Phoebe. My sister always did cook the best.*"

Aunt Elsmere grunted and stared pointedly at Phoebe.

Mama continued, "*Please don't worry about me. I went to Memphis, but had no luck. I ended up getting a ride and went a few hours northeast to a small town outside of Knoxville called Harriman. I met a nice family with the name Brewer who's started their own business with another family called the Millers. It's a store called The 5 to 5, and it's in the biggest building in town. They sell clothing and items ranging anywhere from five cents to five dollars. It's a nice place filled with lots of pretty*" *things—I think Blanche would especially enjoy it. The people are kind and honest, and they have a little girl not much younger than Caroline."*

Caroline frowned. A "little girl" was Phoebe. Not someone old enough to ride on a Ferris wheel with a boy.

"They needed someone to help with the store's accounting. When I told them all about the class I took during my one semester of college, they warmed up to me and I've proven I can do the job. I never imagined this kind of work when I left home. I thought I'd be doing something like I'm used to. But the store makes decent money. I know because the Brewers have saved enough to by themselves a baby grand piano—imagine that, in these hard times!

"I think if I work hard, I can save up easily for a horse or two and a pair of mules in no time. And I hope a little extra to help get us through the winter."

Caroline held her breath. That meant Papa planned to be home in a few short months. *"Here's something to help back at home."* Mama held up five dollars for them to see. Blanche gasped.

"I miss y'all a lot and wish I could be there with y'all now. Please take care of one another and know that I love you so much."

Mama's voice broke. Tears filled her eyes. Her hand shook and she dropped the letter to her lap.

Blanche and Aunt Elsmere frowned at each other. Blanche shrugged. Why was Mama so upset? The letter had been a good one filled with good news. And five dollars.

Later, when Caroline finished working in the fields and came to check on Phoebe before dinner, she crept over to Mama's dresser and picked up Papa's letter from Mama's jewelry box.

She quickly scanned it. Everything was exactly as Mama had read it earlier—except a part at the bottom.

"*P.S.*" it read, "*Marlene, I hate to end on a bad note, but I asked around about George when I was in Memphis the two days before coming here. No word on him. Let me know if y'all find out something before I do. Keep praying.*"

The backs of Caroline's eyes burned. The old wedding photo of Mama and Papa—as young and happy looking as Thomas and Pamelia were now—stared back at her.

No wonder Mama didn't want to read that part to them. It was hard enough reading it, but having to say it out loud would be awful and make Phoebe feel worse.

After all, George had always said when he told the Growing Rock story that if you spoke your hopes and fears out loud, sometimes the fairies had a way of making them come true.

Caroline scraped off a chunk of dried tomato from one of Aunt June's bowls. Disgusting. Tomatoes weren't ever meant to be put into pies.

In the candlelight, the wooden bowl looked perfect and shiny on the outside, but on the inside it was lined with scratches and stains. How many tomato pies had it helped make throughout the years? How many festivals had it been put through?

Aunt June took it from her and rinsed it in the basin of soapy water. "My mama used these bowls before me. And her mother before that." She smiled. "I would pass them onto you, but you don't like tomatoes." The corners of her mouth curled up.

"Can I ask you something?" said Caroline.

"Of course."

Caroline hesitated. "Why don't you and Uncle P. Joe have children?"

Aunt June looked out the window and into the dark sky.

Uh-oh. Maybe that wasn't a smart question. Caroline never thought much about it, but now after learning the family was about to get larger it was hard not to think about babies. Aunt June would've made the perfect mother.

"Caroline, your mama wouldn't be happy that you asked that."

Of course she wouldn't. Mama didn't like questions. Of any sort.

"I know. I'm sorry," Caroline mumbled.

"Don't be sorry. I'm just sayin' she wouldn't like that. *I* don't mind it, and it's my house. I don't see any reason not to answer. It's a perfectly reasonable question."

Aunt June wiped her hands on her apron and returned the bowl for Caroline to dry.

"I had a baby a long time ago. But it died on its third day. It was very small and had problems breathing. It was a little girl. Baby Elsa."

Aunt June sat down at the table. She tapped her feet on the floor as if she had a nervous twitch. "I was pregnant again a few years ago, back when you were much younger. Too young to have noticed I got rather plump."

It was hard to imagine Aunt June ever being plump. She had Caroline's figure, tall and thin.

"But the baby was never born. I miscarried after a few months."

"Oh, I'm so sorry," Caroline whispered.

Aunt June looked up from the floor.

"So am I." She ran her fingers through her wavy red hair. "I never knew if it was a girl or boy. I never had a chance to give it a name. It never made sense why we had problems. We would've been good parents. We wanted a baby more than anyone." Aunt June sighed. "But we *did* have problems, and the doctor thought I'd only have more of them if I kept trying. Now I'm getting too old. I mean, your mama's only a year older than me, and she's got five children. Four of which are pretty done grown. Starting to have kids of their own."

Caroline set the bowl down on the counter with the rest of the dishes Aunt June had used for the festival. "Well, it's never too late."

Aunt June laughed. "Sometimes it is, though. In this case, it is." She shrugged. "But I'm glad I've always gotten to be here for you kids. And it's not too late for me to be a good great-aunt to this new chickadee on the way, now is it?"

"I'm sorry I wasn't at the festival with you today," Caroline said. "And I'm sorry I went with Peter last night. I should've just stayed with you and Phoebe."

Aunt June stood up and untied her apron. "Now don't you apologize. You were at home with Phoebe, where you needed to be today. And you already know how I feel about last night—you had every right to go out and have some fun for once. Besides, what makes you think you being there would stop someone from getting sick?"

She walked down the hall and into the guest room at the front of the house, and Caroline followed. It had never made sense why there was an extra room there, but now it did. It had once been made as a nursery. Now it had a bed for when Aunt June's nephews and nieces came over for a night and a bookshelf filled with lots of books.

Aunt June selected a handful and handed them to Caroline. "I've gotten some new ones lately. Here, take these home. Read them to Phoebe if she feels like it. Maybe we can teach her a few words before she starts school."

If Phoebe was lucky enough to go to school.

The books felt smooth and new, and their covers looked shiny. There were a couple of Agatha Christie mysteries, and a black and white Amelia Earhart stared up at Caroline from the top of one of them called *The Fun of It*.

"That's by Amelia herself, all about her flying experiences. Thought you might enjoy that one. Especially since I heard Elsmere thinks you need to know the differences between an airplane and an air ship." Aunt June's eyes twinkled.

If there was one thing Aunt June didn't' hesitate to spend some extra money on it was books, especially books that she could share with all of them.

Caroline reached up and gave Aunt June a hug. "I hope I'll be half as good of an aunt as you are."

Chapter 8

With Phoebe still feeling sick, and Mama acting all sad-like, Aunt Elsmere insisted on staying inside with them. Which meant extra work both inside and outside for Caroline and Blanche.

Caroline lit a match and started a fire in the stove. She put the rolls of dough inside and shut the door.

It was miserably hot, even with all the windows open.

Blanche entered the kitchen with a large basket of fruits and vegetables. She set it on the table and took her hat off. "Goodness, it's nasty. This humidity is unbearable."

"I know. We've got to go tend the cotton too and instruct the help on where to start."

Blanche ran her fingers through her hair and wiped her face with a damp rag. "I'm not. I gotta go visit Pamelia."

"But Uncle P. Joe's coming later to help us chop. Least we can do is be here so he's not alone."

Blanche shrugged. "I told her I'd come see her. And you just said the colored help is coming."

What was Blanche thinking? Did she not know how much work they had to do? They hardly had any hired help and were falling more and more behind without Papa around. And not even Thomas and Pamelia were there as much now.

"Thomas is with Pamelia. I'm sure she's okay." After all, they'd just found out Pamelia was having a baby. Wouldn't it take a while before she couldn't do things on her own?

Blanche put her hands on her hips. "Honestly. You don't know about babies yet. My friend, Mary-Ella, just had her second one, so I know all about them. It's much more complicated than you realize."

"Well, you need to help me a little bit first."

Blanche patted her on the shoulder. "Don't worry. I'll be back in no time."

Before Caroline could answer, Blanche's hat perched on her head once more, and she strode out the door.

The sun beat down like a whip, scorching Caroline's skin until it felt as if it would melt. She'd be redder than a tomato. She'd be the color of a dark chili pepper. The hot kind that burnt your tongue and made you thirst for a second glass full of water after you'd already gulped one down.

She set the garden hoe beside her feet, next to the huge bag of weeds she'd chopped, and wiped the dampness off her chest with the neckline of her dress. It was already so wet it didn't do much. Her arms stunk underneath, worse than when one of the chickens laid a bad egg. Her braid stuck to the back of her neck. The wisps around her face clung against her forehead.

In that stretch of land, there weren't any trees, just one huge spread of little green plants that would later be full of whiteness. It seemed so big, so endless. And Caroline was just one girl. She hadn't even finished chopping two whole rows of cotton yet. How could she get things ready all by herself before Uncle P. Joe came in for such a short time? How could she even finish the rest of that section?

Caroline tucked her braid inside her hat. She took a deep breath. Then she picked up the hoe and cut a few weeds. It didn't matter if it was only one weed at a time.

She had to do it.

Someone had to get things done. It wasn't fair that Papa had to go away to find work to support them if they weren't going to do their share. It would be for nothing if they didn't try to have things accomplished when he returned.

Maybe it was hopeless to keep wishing George was there. But everything turned out to be a game with him. Even the hardest tasks could be fun if he were around.

Caroline could do this—she could think of some way to make the work better too, just as George had always done. She sat down for a moment to catch her breath. She took her hat off and fanned her face with it.

A few years before, on a day a lot like this, she'd gotten to escape the awful heat.

The sharp bristles on the tops of the plants, just around the fluffy bolls of cotton, scraped her fingers and wrists. The bag weighed half of what she did, if not more. Even in the middle of October, the air was still so warm that day. It felt as if it could've been July.

"I'm hot. And tired," Caroline moaned. "Why can't I go inside with Phoebe?"

"Cause she's four, and you're eleven. You're old enough to help and she's not," Blanche snapped.

Caroline straightened up and just stood there, holding the bag open, while Blanche put handfuls of cotton inside it.

Blanche grabbed Caroline's hands and spread them farther apart. "Hold it open more."

Thomas left his sack a few rows away and came over to them.

"Girls, y'all need to stop your arguing. We got a lot of work to do."

Blanche nodded. "Well, tell Caroline that and not me, cause she's the one who ain't doing nothing. She'll barely hold the bag open."

Thomas took the sack from Caroline and strapped it across her shoulders. She felt herself tilt forward. He took it off and set it down again. "Maybe it's cause it's heavier than she is. It will hold upright by itself after a while. Here, Caroline, you pick too. You'll get more done that way."

He wiped his forehead on a battered handkerchief from his overalls pocket and watched her.

Caroline grabbed some of the white fluffiness, but the stems of the plants cut into her fingertips like little paper cuts. She felt her eyes fill with tears. It was too hot to be picking cotton. It was too hot to do anything, and her head hurt.

In the distance, George caught her attention. He grinned and rolled his eyes at Thomas.

They never got along much. Thomas, always so serious, and George, always the playful one.

When Thomas went to the other side of the field to help Papa hang a big sack of cotton on the skinny metal hook of the cotton scale, George came over.

He whispered in her ear so Blanche couldn't hear. "Don't worry about them. We'll be done soon, and we'll have a surprise, just me and you when we're done."

Caroline's eyes grew wide. She'd finally discover where George escaped to almost every afternoon.

"George, you should've told me we were coming this far. I would've fixed my hair and worn my Sunday dress." Caroline tried smoothing her braid. She put her arms down because they smelled so bad.

"Heck, no, you wouldn't have. Or I wouldn't have brought you. You think Mama wouldn't notice you wearing a good dress?"

"Well, where are we—"

"Shhh."

They'd come to the town square with all the brick buildings and the enormous cannon from the Civil War that was displayed right in the middle of it all, sparkling in the sunlight. They walked past the store Mama liked to buy material at, Berg and Schaefer, and past Nelson's Hardware. They paused across the street from the movie theater, The Webb. It felt weird to be there in town and not dressed up.

"What are we—"

"If I gotta keep tellin' you to hush, this ain't gonna work." George grabbed her arm and walked real fast to a door on the side of the theater. He tapped twice.

His friend Robert answered.

He took one glance at Caroline and shook his head. "Nah, that ain't part of the deal."

Before he could close it, George caught the door in his hand. "I'll invite you over all day tomorrow after church."

Robert's face turned red. "Really?" He cleared his throat. "Will, uh, you know. Will she be there?"

George grinned. "You bet. She's making delicious blueberry pies later today. Heard her talkin' earlier about a new dress she's wearing to church."

They must've been talking about Blanche. Of course. Who else could make Robert have that silly look on his face?

Robert let the door open more. He sighed and glanced around. "Oh, all right. She ain't the kind of kiddo to cause problems anyhow. Just this once."

George nudged Caroline inside. They entered a small hallway. Robert opened a door.

"Slide in the back and don't make no noise," Robert whispered. "See ya Sunday." He looked George square in the eye, as if putting a seal on their deal.

The room grew very dark, except for some small lights lining the walkway. A large screen that was as tall as their home stood before them. Above them, in a little room behind all the seats, a bright light shone onto the screen. A man wound a handle back and forth.

"That's to unwind the film," George explained. "Wanna see something cool?" He stood up and reached a hand into the air. A giant shadow of a hand appeared on the screen. All the heads in front of them turned around.

Caroline giggled. Phoebe would love making shadow puppets on this wall.

Robert hadn't left. He snuck up behind them and wacked George on the head with his hand. "No more of that," he hissed. "It's taken me forever to get this job. You attract attention, and they'll know you didn't buy tickets."

The room grew quiet. The lights darkened to almost pitch black. A Mickey Mouse cartoon appeared before them. Caroline snuggled down into the seat. It felt soft and comfy. And somehow being in the dark, surrounded by people who were all so excited, it didn't seem hot at all.

So this was where George disappeared to after those long hours in the fields. They'd all been too tired to notice he was gone. Except for her, of course.

That explained why Robert came over all the time for dinner, trying to talk to Blanche and get her to go dancing with him. It was an exchange for George's free movies.

Poor thing. Maybe someday Blanche would agree to go out with him.

The music began, and a sweet story about flying and a little girl, played by Shirley Temple, who'd lost her mother, began to unfold.

It was Caroline's first movie.

"Caroline, Caroline, are you okay?"

Caroline opened her eyes. She was in bed with nothing on but her thin, white slip.

"What happened?"

Aunt Elsmere hovered inches away from her face, searching without blinking, as if they were playing a staring game.

"Peter happened to be coming over to check on things and found you lying down in the fields. You fainted from the heat."

Caroline reached up to touch her forehead, where there was a cold, wet rag. And something was inside that rag. Something small and kind of crunchy.

Aunt Elsmere propped the cloth back on Caroline's forehead. "It's ice," she said. "Peter bought it for you a little while ago when the ice man came by."

What a perfect day to sell ice. But where was Peter?

"Hold still," Aunt Elsmere said when Caroline tried sitting up.

"Where is he?"

Aunt Elsmere stiffened. "I sent him on home."

"After giving him leftover tomato pie, of course," she quickly added. Caroline's eyes must've grown large at the words "sent him on."

"He said he'll stop by tomorrow to check on you." Aunt Elsmere sighed. "Now why on earth did you let yourself get that overheated that you passed out?"

As if anyone could control the temperature.

"I'm sorry. I didn't mean to."

"Well, next time, drink more water." Aunt Elsmere closed the curtains so the room was dark. "Enough work for today. Get some rest." On her way out she mumbled, "Another body to take care of."

Caroline took the rag off her forehead and plopped one of the ice chips on her tongue. It dissolved after only a second, but it tasted so nice and cold. She ate the rest of the melting ice and lifted her slip up so she could spread the wet rag across her belly.

What did Peter think of her for fainting? Did he think she was weak? Or like a little girl still?

He did buy her the ice, though, so he must have been worried.

Caroline ran her fingers over the thin slip. Did he see her wearing this? Hopefully not because it was basically nothing. She put a hand over her chest. It would be embarrassing for him to see how small she was. Lying down made her look even smaller.

But it was Aunt Elsmere who'd tended to her. So of course he hadn't seen anything.

She closed her eyes.

"Can I please leave my room? Honestly, I'm fine."

Aunt Elsmere lifted her left eyebrow, the way she did whenever she got suspicious about something.

"I promise I'm okay."

"Okay isn't passing out when you're only fourteen."

"That was hours ago. I was only overheated."

Aunt Elsmere didn't budge. She stood there with her arms crossed, eyebrow still raised.

Caroline sighed. "Look, I even ate all the soup you brought me." She held up her empty bowl.

Actually, she'd opened her window and tossed the soup out into the bushes below. It was an awful thing to do, to waste food. But it wasn't much of a waste. They'd be eating tomatoes for days. Days and days. They always did after the Tomato Festival. And why would anyone want tomato soup if she didn't like tomatoes to begin with? Besides, food was the only way to convince Aunt Elsmere she was feeling better so she could leave her room.

Aunt Elsmere grabbed the empty bowl and peered into it. "Well, I'm glad someone likes my cooking. There's plenty of more where this came from."

Caroline groaned on the inside. "Great. Can I go to Mama's room and see Phoebe?" Before Aunt Elsmere answered, she added, "I'll try to get her to eat, too."

Perfect. The eyebrows completely relaxed. "Okay. I suppose so. I'm going outside to sit on the porch with your mother now."

Once inside Mama's room, Caroline sat at the edge of the bed. It looked so big and Phoebe so small. Phoebe had shifted to the middle, so at least Papa's side wasn't quite as lumpy as before.

Phoebe stirred her spoon around in her bowl of soup.

"You know if you just eat even some of that, Aunt Elsmere will leave you alone more."

"But it's terrible."

"I thought you liked tomatoes."

"I do, but this is still terrible."

Caroline sighed. "Try eating just a little."

Phoebe took a bite and made a face. She held her nose the way Blanche did sometimes and ate a few spoonfuls very fast.

"That's a good girl." Caroline walked over to Mama's jewelry box. Where was Papa's letter? She'd wanted to read that part about George again. She opened the bottom drawer and sifted through the various letters and cards Mama had saved. Since Mama hardly had any jewelry, it was more of a mailbox than anything else.

Caroline's breath caught in her throat. At the bottom of the stack was an envelope titled "George" in Mama's tiny handwriting. Inside it were several letters. The letters he'd written months ago before they all of a sudden stopped coming.

The floorboards on the old stairs creaked.

Caroline stuffed the envelope underneath her nightgown. She slammed the jewelry box lid down.

Phoebe took a big mouthful of soup and almost choked as she gulped it.

Mama came in. She paid no attention to Phoebe's proud display of the empty bowl. Her eyes seemed unfocused. Her hair was a mess.

Had Mama just been sitting in the kitchen staring out the window with that blank, far-off expression again? What had she been doing all day while her sister had taken care of them?

"Girls, I'm getting ready to go to bed."

Phoebe frowned at Caroline. It wasn't even completely dark yet.

Mama started putting on her nightgown. Caroline and Phoebe both stared. It was hard not to. Mama's stomach had shrunken and her rib cage poked out a bit, the way Phoebe's did. Some of the skin around the tops of her legs hung kind of loose, like the edges of a half-filled cotton sack.

Mama had never undressed in front of them before. She'd always been very cautious about such things. Not quite like Aunt Elsmere, but cautious. Now, she just unfastened all of her garments, as if no one else were around.

It was too bad Phoebe couldn't stay in another room, but Aunt Elsmere had taken over the small extra room, and Mama wouldn't ever let her stay in the boys' old room. If she did, it would mean that she, too, was admitting George wasn't coming back.

The pack of letters began to slide from under Caroline's armpit. The corner of the envelope poked her side. She crossed her arms tightly to stop it from falling out on the floor. Even though, with the way Mama was acting she probably wouldn't notice if it did.

"Goodnight, y'all." Caroline yawned, pretending to be exhausted still.

On her way back to the bedroom, Aunt Elsmere passed by.

"Phoebe ate everything," Caroline said.

"Well, I'm glad." Aunt Elsmere rubbed her eyes. Had she been crying? She straightened up quickly. "I tell you what. Your mama's got me worried. I ain't never seen her this depressed. Shoulda known your Pa was gonna do this to her one day. I'd always had a gut feeling."

What was Aunt Elsmere talking about? Did she think he wasn't coming back?

Caroline felt the color drain from her face. "Papa wouldn't 'do' anything to Mama on purpose that'd hurt her. He's coming back soon. His letter said so."

Aunt Elsmere grunted. "You know as well as I do your Pa has his ways of trying to make everyone feel good and keep their chins up. Fact is he's done gone much farther than what he'd said."

It had gotten a lot darker in the last couple of minutes. In the hallway, it was hard to see, but surely Aunt Elsmere had that awful smirk on her face. It was unbearable. How could she doubt Papa that way?

Without another word, Caroline opened the bedroom door and went in. It was so warm in there, and Blanche was gone— still gone from that morning.

Caroline took a blanket downstairs and went on the back porch, where it was much cooler with the air coming through the screen.

Even in the candlelight, she easily could read George's familiar handwriting.

The first one was from January 15th.

Dear everyone back home,

Hope ya'll are doing as well as I am. I've been in Memphis the last few days doing odd jobs here and there. Met a lot of nice people and have had plenty to eat soup kitchens ain't as bad as people have said. Not anything like your cookin Mama, but don't worry, I won't come home skin and bones.

Here's something to help out.
Xoxo,
George

The letter had had a dollar in it. Enough to buy Phoebe's first bottle of cough syrup. The next was from January 22nd.

Dear family,

You should see the way a city lights up at night. Sure is different from our starry skies back home. Actually everything is different from back home.

Sorry to hear about Phoebe being sick. Did the doc say if it's turned to pnewmonia? Sounds like she may just have a bad touch of the flu. It's going around. Here's a few extra dollars to help. Buy some thick wool to make her a better blanket and give her a hug for me.

Love always,
George

Caroline slowly folded the letter back. She'd gone into town with Aunt June one day and brought the letter back from the post office. It felt like a long time ago when she thought about how excited she'd been to get home and read it with everyone.

But now it all seemed odd. Odd that his letters were so short. Odd that he never explained what jobs he was doing and never described the people he met.

If any of them had a knack for making up a story, it was George. He could spin a tale out of anything. So why had he sent such brief letters with little information? After all, he'd wanted to get out of Ripley and go somewhere his whole life. He said being away was "different," but in a good way or bad way?

The third and final letter had been written February 12th. It had been a cold day when it arrived. Phoebe had been sick, worse than before, and that letter, unlike the others, had made Caroline feel sad and hopeless.

To my family back home,

Times are hard. I know we all know that, and for you young'uns, you were just born into the world hearing that. But even so I never knew how hard things are until I got out on my own. Everywhere I go, I see the same worried hungry faces. Different faces of course but always worried and hungry.

Sure, it's tough in Ripley with people not being able to pay mortgages and having to sell off their land, but that ain't nothin' compared to some stories I've heard. Stories about the dust storms out west that are so powerful they just suffocate you and tear down your home. Or stories about families havin' to give their children away and send them on an orphan train cause they can't feed 'em. We have things rough, but I guess I'm just learning they can always be worse.

The rivers have been flooding an awful lot. I've gone to different areas tryin' to escape it. The whole neighborhood I was in just the other night was all but destroyed yesterday. As if things ain't bad enough, the very earth itself seems to be punishing us, what with dust storms and floods. I can't help wonder, why?

I'm so sorry to hear about Phoebe. Once the water goes down, I'll try to head on back. Not much a body can do to earn money anywhere now anyway, unless you wanna go north or somethin'.

Miss you lots,
George

The cot squeaked underneath Caroline as she laid down. George had clearly wanted to come back. What had stopped him? The floods that continued after that?

They'd all understood what George meant by saying he was coming home. He'd wanted to tell Phoebe goodbye because she didn't seem as if she'd get better. How could he not come home, then, unless something awful had happened? Why would he just stop writing, unless something had gone wrong?

But then again, maybe there was more to it. His letters were so brief, so lacking in details. It didn't seem right. Maybe Robert knew something. He'd been George's friend since they were little kids. Longer than Caroline had been friends with Peter. Maybe she could ask Robert and get some new ideas.

Caroline put the letters under her pillow. She crept through the darkness and down the hill, the grass tickling her bare feet, and sat on the Growing Rock. She curled her legs up to her chest with her nightgown stretched over them and hugged herself in a ball.

The stars George claimed he missed stared down at her.

A sound louder than the crickets and frogs grew stronger. On the road a car stopped and turned off its headlights. A moment later the lights came back on and Blanche ran up toward the house. Her blouse hung loosely off one of her shoulders. Her hair looked tangled, even in the dark. But she was smiling, giggling softly, her teeth white as the stars.

Now where had she been all day? Whose car was that? Did it belong to that friend of Robert's? Had Blanche gone somewhere without him?

Caroline uncurled herself and stretched against the smoothest part of the rock. Her legs still didn't quite reach the end of it.

Maybe if she stayed there all night, she'd grow along with it.

Chapter 9

"Don't give me anymore of that nonsense." Aunt Elsmere stood there with one hand on her hip, one hand shaking a spoon, and a big scowl on her face. The buttons right underneath the straps of her apron looked as if they would pop off at any moment.

Caroline sighed. Not much use in arguing anymore. If Aunt Elsmere wanted her to go work for a crazy squirrel killer, she'd just have to do it. Mama wouldn't have made her go if she paid attention. But Mama wasn't herself at all lately, and Aunt Elsmere was taking advantage of it.

"You're going, and that's that." Aunt Elsmere gave the spoon one final tap in the air toward Caroline. Gravy dripped onto the floor. "And clean that up." She turned around to the hot pot of gravy and stirred it a little too rough. The creamy mess splattered from the pot and burned Aunt Elsmere's fingers. She put her fingertips in her mouth to cool them, her face bright pink.

Caroline squatted on her hands and knees and scrubbed up the spill with a wet rag. It was stupid to say anything more, not when Aunt Elsmere was in this kind of mood. And, for once, her grumpiness was kind of understandable. Mama wasn't hardly doing anything these days. She was about like a scarecrow, pretty much useless and just taking up space. It was mean to think that, but it was the truth. Aunt Elsmere acted more like a mother for Phoebe than Mama. She'd tended to everything for her the entire week.

Blanche entered the kitchen, just barely avoiding stepping on Caroline's hand. "Auntie, I'm going to see Elsa May."

Aunt Elsmere raised her spoon and slung more gravy on the floor. "Aren't you gonna help Caroline? She's gotta go to

Miss Evelyn's later today, so I can't spare both of you."

"I'll be back before she leaves." Blanche tore off a piece of bacon from the plate on the counter and nibbled it. "Elsa May needs help with her two babies, now that her man's gone."

"Well, all right then. Guess that's okay."

Caroline set the glasses on the table. She reached for a piece of the bacon.

Aunt Elsmere slapped her hand. "Wait until we're at the table and have said 'Grace'," she said.

The sound of the wood splitting always made Caroline think about flying. It was loud and fast, the ax swinging through the air, cutting into the tree trunk with full force. Maybe that was kind of the way it sounded when Amelia Earhart's plane took off. Slow at first, then faster and faster until all of a sudden it sprung from the ground only to hit nothing, just air alone.

And it was comforting.

Peter's whole face gleamed with perspiration. The white shirt underneath his overalls showed wet spots in the arm holes. His muscles shone through the shirt when he lifted his arms.

He pulled the ax from the tree and swung it over his head once more. It hit the tree with a force strong enough to finish the cut that split it into two.

"Geez, it's doggone hot." He wiped his face with a handkerchief and set the ax down.

Caroline moved over on the log where she was sitting to make room for him. "Well, thanks to you we can use our stoves and cook lots of meals later on."

Peter grinned but didn't sit down. "Guess that means I'll be invited for supper?"

The heat rose all the way to Caroline's hairline. By the time that wood was seasoned enough to burn, what would things be like between the two of them?

Peter stretched out on the grass across from her, pulling his hat over his face. "I'll be. Even in the shade, I betchya it's a hundred degrees today. I hope this rain hurries up."

Caroline sighed. Sure enough, it looked as if it would pour any moment. "I'll check Miss Evelyn's thermometer just for you."

He pulled the hat up and looked at her with one eye. "So you're going back, eh?"

"Yeah, unfortunately. Not much of a chance to escape, is there? My Mama is acting worse. Like one of 'em sick cows, off by herself, not sayin' much, not eatin' much." Caroline pulled a piece of bark off the log. "And with Phoebe being so weak still, guess I kinda owe it to my aunt to just do it, you know?"

Peter nodded, the cap over his face again.

Caroline twirled the bark in her fingers. "Guess I better head on over there before it rains. She'll be expecting me soon."

"Wait." Peter stood up and brushed his pant legs off. Was he going to walk her there? Was he going to ask to see her later?

Instead, he reached for her hand. He gave it a small squeeze that made her suddenly shiver in the heat.

"It'll be okay," Peter said. "See you later."

Words caught in Caroline's throat. "Good bye," she finally managed to croak.

But Peter was already lost in the shadows of the trees.

The thunder sounded like many axes that were striking the thickest trees with the heaviest force. The gravel road looked like a small river with the rain moving along it.

"Step away from that window," Miss Evelyn stuttered. She held onto one of her cats, an orange one the color of a pale pumpkin. "You'll get electrocuted."

Caroline backed away. A brown cat squealed and ran out of the room.

"Watch where you step."

"Sorry. Maybe I can turn on some lights?"

Miss Evelyn shook her head. "No, I don't want to get electrocuted."

"I'll light some more candles then." Caroline had to hold onto the kitchen counter so she wouldn't trip in the semi-darkness. What was the point of having electricity if you couldn't use it during a storm? Why would anyone want it if it meant you got electrocuted when it rained? Peter had never mentioned that you couldn't use it if there was lightening.

Once a few candles were lit, Caroline regretted it. The house seemed messier even than she remembered it. The door to the hallway was now open and clutter junked up the space everywhere she looked. It seemed as if Miss Evelyn had cleared a path just to get from one room to the next. Newspapers, empty bottles, boxes, and old clothes were everywhere, like a forest of clutter.

The house smelled like one big wet cat. They'd all been outside the last time. Now they sat around Miss Evelyn, like scared children, purring.

Too bad it didn't look as if it was going to quit raining. Working in a tomato garden or doing laundry would have at least made the time go by.

Miss Evelyn's head rested sidewise in her chair. The thunder boomed, the house shook, and she jolted upright and wiped some drool from the corner of her mouth.

"I was just about to doze off," she said. "Well, since you're here and you can't clean in the dark, can you read to me?"

"Yes, ma'am—what would you like me to read?"

Miss Evelyn picked her Bible up from the china cabinet by the table. It was the same one she'd shaken at Caroline and Peter. "This is always a good choice."

Caroline opened it up. "Which story would you like to hear?"

Miss Evelyn stroked the orange cat. "How about Noah and the flood, since it's raining?"

The gold clock shimmered in the candlelight. Only twenty minutes had passed. But Caroline could do it. She could stay and read out loud to an old lady. It would be just like Jo reading to her Great Aunt March in *Little Women*. She'd been a grouchy old lady, too. But Jo had managed. If Jo could do it, Caroline could too.

Slowly, she opened the book to Genesis.

The Bible, resting on Caroline's lap, almost fell off. She'd reached the part about the dove bringing Noah the olive branch when Miss Evelyn's dozing had turned into a loud, deep snore. Caroline caught the book before it could fall and break the spell.

With Miss Evelyn sleeping, it was almost peaceful, even in that awful house, sitting there in the darkness, just listening to the rain. For once, she wasn't having to do anything, or listen to anyone telling her to do something or reminding her of what she'd have to do the next day. She could sit there and do absolutely nothing.

But, of course, it was a waste not to do anything. Jo always found something interesting to do when her reading lulled Great Aunt March to sleep.

Caroline gently set the Bible on a stack of newspapers. She tiptoed to avoid stepping on one of the cats and made her way down the hallway. Miss Evelyn had stacked the clutter so high against the walls, it felt suffocating. She was about to turn around when she came to a door that looked as if it might lead to Miss Evelyn's bedroom.

A shiver suddenly went through her body. What would Peter say when she told him she got to see Miss Evelyn's room? What sorts of things were in there? More garbage? Jars of those awful pickles? Squirrels hanging by their tails from the ceiling?

Caroline pushed the halfway shut door open even more. Sure enough, a pile of empty jars stacked on more newspapers rested on the right side of the door. She stepped a couple of feet inside and sighed. Nothing very special. Just a bed with a plain white quilt, a dresser painted a soft shade of green and a bookshelf crammed with books. A little chest sat underneath the window in the corner of the room.

She glanced down the hallway. No sound, except the rain. Miss Evelyn and her cats had to be asleep still. She moved toward the chest and squatted down to open it.

The air smelled like mildew as soon as the lid came up. She reached down and felt a bunch of papers. It was probably only more newspapers or magazine cutouts.

But it wasn't trash this time. It was old photographs printed on thin pieces of tin. Old tintypes like the kind Aunt Elsmere brought with her. They were of people Caroline didn't recognize.

She pulled more of the photos out of the chest until she came to one with a man and a lady and two small children. The little girl wore a fancy dress that came all the way up to her neck, like Mama had said was the fashion when her mother was young. It was a good thing the style had changed. Wearing dresses like those would be miserable in this heat. The lady's dress must've been worse. It had a huge collar and looked all stiff in the middle, as if it was squeezing her stomach. Was she Miss Evelyn? She was so much cleaner and prettier. Her hair sat on the top of her head, full and shiny, not anything like the thin, greasy strands that hung limp around her face now. But she had the same eyes.

Only these eyes had a glow to them, their own kind of smile. No one in the photo smiled. People in the photos hardly ever did because it took so long to take the picture.

Yet there was a difference between the lady's stillness and the man's. Behind her seriousness was a warmth, a friendliness in the way she touched the youngest child's shoulder, the way she slightly tilted her head to the right. The man's eyes looked dark. He held his hands behind his back. Maybe it was the thick suit. If it was anything like the weather now, he probably felt like fainting.

Underneath that photo was a letter, crumbled and yellowed. Caroline paused. Would it be wrong to read someone else's letters? Surely Miss Evelyn didn't want anyone seeing them if they were in a chest. But Caroline had already seen the photos.

Without another thought, she opened it.

December 23, 1892

Dear sister,

I'm so sorry about what you had to say in your last letter. To think that you, only twenty-five and still so young, have had to deal with what you've faced lately is an utter shame! I spoke with Father Grissom about it during Confession last week. He sat there, quite solemn, and thought for a long time. When he did speak, he said that gluttony is a terrible sin, especially when it changes one so and makes things difficult for others. But he also said that you shouldn't blame yourself. I agree. You can only encourage John and try to go on as normal, but you yourself can't change him. Only he can do so, with the Lord's help.

Please try, even if you can't for yourself, but for the children's sakes, to have a pleasant time this Christmas. I wish you could come be here in Boston with all of us for the holidays like always, but since you can't, please do make the best of it all with your own family. Give Harry and Emma my love.

> *Love Always,*
> *Gertrude*

Thoughts raced through Caroline's mind. It seemed as if she'd read a section of a book and wanted to finish it. Who was Gertrude? Was she writing to Miss Evelyn? Was John the name of her husband? What had happened between her and John? Did the family have a good Christmas after all?

It was too bad Caroline couldn't read more of the yellowed papers at the bottom of the trunk. But it would be unwise to continue. Not when so much time had passed. How long had she been gone? If Miss Evelyn woke up, she'd be in trouble for snooping. Then she'd never know what had happened to the people in that letter.

When she tiptoed back to the den, Miss Evelyn was still snoring, her head hanging to her right side. The orange cat in her lap slept too, curled in her arms like a baby. Her fingers rested on its back, gently, lovingly, as if she'd been stroking it when she fell asleep.

There was something familiar about it. The lady in the photo had her hand on the little girl's shoulder in the same exact way.

The rain finally stopped. The clock said it was already past four o'clock. But Caroline sat there a few minutes longer so Miss Evelyn would have someone there when she woke up.

Maybe Miss Evelyn was kind of the way Mama had been lately, faded and "lost her bloom," as Aunt Elsmere would say.

Like a rainbow after a storm, bright at first, then faded into nothing.

Chapter 10

Blanche held her nightgown high enough that you could see her panties. She moved her right foot in front of her and her left foot behind her. She glided forward, forward, back, back, kicking her legs to the sides with a sharp jerk from the knee down. She took a step, a kick, and then moved one hand down to the floor, keeping in time with "Sweet Georgia Brown." The floorboards creaked beneath her.

Phoebe giggled. She held onto the bedpost and tried to do what Blanche had done. Blanche clapped her hands and shouted, "One, two, three and four, five, six, seven, eight."

Caroline flopped down on the bed. Her face felt flushed, and the room had grown even hotter than before. Maybe it was a good thing she hadn't gotten to dance at the Bisbee Show because she couldn't even get the Charleston right.

Phoebe's legs moved fast, her feet turned the right way, and she could follow along with Blanche's counting. She'd surely be a good dancer in no time, just like Blanche.

They'd, no doubt, wake up Mama and Aunt Elsmere, but neither Blanche nor Caroline moved to turn the music off. It was too much fun watching Phoebe hold the bedpost and dance the Charleston, making shadows scatter across the room in the light of the oil lamp. For the first time in two weeks, all three of them were staying in their bedroom.

"Don't stop dancing, Caroline!" Blanche continued kicking her feet out and half walked, half danced toward her.

Phoebe giggled. She went to the dresser and changed stations on the radio. Fred Astaire's softer voice now filled the room.

"Heaven, I'm in Heaven," Phoebe sang, her scratchy voice off-key. Her curls stuck out in every direction. She hummed because she didn't know all the words. "Dancing cheek to cheek."

Blanche hopped on the bed with Caroline and tossed a pillow at her.

Caroline threw the pillow back at Blanche and laughed. "This song's not right for the Charleston. It's way too slow!"

They both bounced up anyhow, and each grabbed one of Phoebe's hands. They all moved in a circle, tripping over one another's feet and laughing till their sides ached.

"Goodness gracious." Aunt Elsmere's frame blocked the doorway. "Why look how pale Phoebe's face is. Not even one night, and y'all have done exhausted her already. I shoulda known not to let her leave her Mama's room yet."

Blanche let go of Phoebe's hand. Caroline felt Phoebe stagger and held onto her from behind. She hugged her from around her shoulders. "Auntie, Phoebe's just fine. We were just trying to do the dance Mama and Papa did when they first met. Papa always says it's good for her to move around and get some exercise."

Aunt Elsmere grunted. "Then maybe Papa should get home and say it himself." She turned the radio off. "Don't waste the batteries on this kind of nonsense. Now go to bed, all of you." She moved toward the window. "And keep this closed. Phoebe will never get over a summer cold if it's open."

Caroline groaned. After dancing and moving, her nightgown stuck to her bare back. Her underwear clung to the tops of her legs and in her bottom.

Aunt Elsmere shut the door. Phoebe laughed and let go of Caroline. She jumped on the bed and rolled to the middle, her favorite place to sleep. "Next time you go dancing, Blanche, can I come?"

Blanche smiled and moved toward the closet. She pulled her nightgown off and threw on one of her Sunday dresses. "Not tonight."

What did Blanche mean? It had to be half-past nine already. Blanche's eyes met Caroline's. "I'm going to see Robert, okay?"

"Now?"

"Yes, now."

"But it's almost your curfew already."

"Yeah, so? Just don't tell Mama, all right?"

Caroline crossed her arms. Of course she wouldn't tell Mama. For as long as she could remember, there'd been an agreement with the kids of the family. You didn't tell on each other. You just didn't, unless, of course, it was something really important. It made things easier for everybody. Plus, Mama didn't care about anything going on anymore anyway.

"I wanna go!" Phoebe wailed.

Between Caroline and Blanche, of course Blanche was the one Phoebe wanted to be just like. It didn't matter that Caroline was the one who always did things to take care of her. Blanche made everything in her life look like one big dance of fun.

Blanche kissed the top of Phoebe's head. "You will soon, love. I promise I'll take you soon." Blanche opened the window and climbed out on the roof. "Leave the window cracked for me, won't you, Caroline?" She held onto the drainage pipe and slid down into the flower bushes beneath.

Caroline crawled into bed next to Phoebe. It looked as if they'd be sleeping with the window open, after all.

The next morning, Blanche wasn't in the bedroom. Caroline helped Phoebe get dressed and braided her hair. When they got downstairs, there was Blanche in her checkered apron fixing breakfast. She stirred the eggs with one hand and the biscuit batter with another.

"Oh, there you two are. It's almost seven o'clock. I was wonderin' if y'all would *ever* wake up." She handed the bowl of batter to Phoebe. "Stir, please," she said. She turned to Caroline. "Can you fetch some more wood for the stove?"

Before Caroline could answer, Peter walked in the kitchen, his arms loaded with a stack of wood.

"Why, thank you, Peter." Blanche took the wood out of his arms and gave him a sweet smile. Peter's face turned pink.

"You're welcome," he muttered.

Blanche turned back to the eggs. Why did she have to look so pretty every morning? Why did that blasted apron have to fit so perfectly around her tiny waist? And where had she been last night? Had she even come home to sleep?

Caroline ran her fingers through her hair, still down and matted. She hadn't even brushed it yet because she'd been so focused on helping Phoebe. Her breath probably smelled awful, too. It tasted as if she'd just eaten a bad tomato.

Peter finally tore his eyes away from Blanche and spotted her. "Hello."

"Hello." Caroline stirred the batter for Phoebe. "I didn't know you were coming or I would've gotten up earlier." She would've gotten up earlier *and* fixed her hair.

"It's okay. I've just been here a few minutes. My dad didn't need me helping with anything." He shrugged. "Thought I'd come see how y'all were doing." He patted Phoebe on the head. "Glad you're feelin' better. I worried about you."

Phoebe smiled. "Thank you. I'm hungry again."

"Well, that's good. Do you wanna come over with Caroline later? I had something I wanted to show y'all."

"If she feels like it, she can go," Aunt Elsmere said, entering the kitchen. She opened the wooden door so the screen door to the porch was open. She fanned her face. "My, it's so hot already. Glad you came by today, Peter. I don't want any of my nieces fainting."

Her eyes met Caroline's, and she gave her a small smile.

Somehow, Peter had found his way back on Aunt Elsmere's good side.

That whole day, Peter hardly said a word to Caroline. She'd planned on telling him about Miss Evelyn's trunk and asking what he thought of it all, but every time she tried talking, he didn't say much and just kept working on whatever Aunt Elsmere wanted.

Had Aunt Elsmere said something to him? Surely not. Not when she'd made a point to smile at Caroline before breakfast. And when would she have had time? Aunt Elsmere hadn't seen him since the day Caroline fainted.

And Peter was over his Blanche heartbreak. He'd been over that for a long time. Ever since Blanche got engaged and stayed engaged, all the other boys in Ripley stopped trying to win her over. There was harmless flirting, of course, but it seemed like nothing more.

Then what was it? Caroline hadn't done anything wrong. Peter didn't seem mad, exactly, but distant. And—awkward.

Caroline left Peter and the cotton fields to hoe the vegetable garden by herself. By the time she was finished, Peter was sitting on the porch swinging with Phoebe.

She stopped and wiped her forehead. Why was he laughing and talking to Phoebe, but he had had nothing to say to her, his closest friend?

He quit talking when she walked up the steps.

Phoebe jumped off the swing. "Caroline, Peter wants to show us something. Can we go?"

"Sure. I guess so."

The three of them walked on the path beside the cotton field that led from the Neal farm to Peter's house. It was easier that way and avoided the dust of the road on their shoes.

Phoebe went on and on about the Charleston, but Peter didn't say much, so Caroline hardly said anything either. Would Peter have talked more if she hadn't been there? What was the point of even inviting them?

The sun shone with a fierceness that made Caroline's head ache. When they reached Peter's house they were all so thirsty that Peter's mother made them a fresh pitcher of sweet tea.

Caroline always forgot how grand Peter's home seemed. It wasn't too much larger than theirs, but they had electricity. Papa had once said they had paid for their property in full, and so they could afford more than some people around because they didn't have mortgages to pay.

And Peter was the oldest of seven, and the only boy, not one of the youngest in a family of five like Caroline. He didn't get treated like a little kid the way she sometimes was. His Mama was still nursing the youngest one, a baby named Ida.

"Let's go to the barn," Peter said. "I wanna show you what's in there."

"The barn?" Phoebe wrinkled her face. "I thought we were trying to get away from work, not do more."

Peter grinned and rolled his eyes. "You'll see."

In the corner of the barn, one big gray cat was feeding a new litter of five kittens. They were tiny balls of gray, so small they fit perfectly in the palm of Peter's hand.

"Oh, how cute!" Phoebe squealed.

They really were precious. Not yet big and smelly like Miss Evelyn's cats. These had a fresh smell to them, like a newborn baby. They nestled in the hay, getting as close to their mother as possible.

Annie and Debra Jean, both close to Phoebe's age, ran into the barn.

"Phoebe," Annie, the older of the two said, "Come play tea party with us."

"Ma gave us some cookies to go with the tea," Debra Jean said.

Phoebe looked up at Caroline. "Can I?"

Caroline nodded. "For a little bit. Aunt June's coming later, so we need to be back soon."

Without another word, Phoebe skipped over to the other girls and disappeared around the corner. Now that she felt better, Phoebe wanted to do everything and went from one thing to the next fast. Her attention didn't stay on anything long.

Peter rubbed the mother cat and didn't look at Caroline.

Caroline sighed and sat on an upside down milk bucket. One of the kittens purred at her feet. She picked it up. It felt so soft and light, probably only a couple of pounds, if that.

"I can't believe how tiny they are."

Peter nodded. "They'll grow up in no time."

"Plenty of mice around to fatten them up, I guess."

Peter's eyes finally met hers. He looked sheepish, like he had with Blanche that morning, as if he was embarrassed by something. With Blanche, it was because everyone knew he'd liked her for a long time. With Caroline, it made no sense. They'd been best friends forever.

Maybe he was embarrassed he'd held her hand at the Bisbee Show. Maybe he didn't want her thinking too much on it, but didn't know what to say.

Caroline's own face felt flushed. She focused on the kitten in her lap. It licked her fingers with its tiny pink tongue. When she looked back up, Peter was watching her.

"You should keep that kitten," he said.

"Really? You mean it?"

"Course I do. We got seven kids here and plenty of animals. The last thing we really need is more animals to care for. Phoebe will love it."

"Maybe Mama will too." Caroline had said it before she'd thought about it. The words had just come out. But maybe Mama *would* like a kitten. Something new and small to care for, something to get her mind off of things.

"Well, you can take him as soon as he grows up a little. We don't wanna take him from his Ma too soon."

"Oh, it's a *boy*." Caroline giggled. "Well, we could definitely use some more boys in the house."

Caroline and Phoebe came in through the front door and walked back to the kitchen, but they stopped at the foot of the stairs.

"Shh," Caroline said, putting her finger in front of her lips. For some reason, she just knew they didn't need to walk in at the moment. The door to the kitchen was cracked a few inches. Phoebe sat on the bottom step. Caroline hunched down beside her so they wouldn't be seen.

Mama sat at her spot at the kitchen table. Now that she sat there so often they called it "Mama's spot." She held some papers in her hand and stared at them. Aunt June sat beside her with a basket of muffins she brought over.

"Here, dear, have a blueberry muffin. It will make you feel better," Aunt June coaxed.

Mama shook her head.

Aunt June sighed. "Well, I know how you feel. It's hard to do much of anything when you're feeling down, but not eating is only going to make you ill. You've gotten so thin. You really need to eat."

Mama shook her head again.

Aunt June gently took the papers from Mama's hand and set them at the other end of the table. She placed a muffin on a napkin in front of Mama. Mama didn't even seem to see it, but Aunt June broke it into small pieces for her.

"I know it's hard to lose a child," she said softly, almost in a whisper. "I know what it feels like. It happened in a different way for me, but I know."

Phoebe frowned. "What's she talking about?" she whispered.

"Hush," Caroline said. "Just listen."

Mama then snapped out of her trance. She pushed the muffin away, knocking it on the floor. "You *don't* know. You don't know anything." Mama's voice rose. Her eyes were red. "The children you lost never had names, you never had memories of them, you never took care of them when they were sick or bought presents for them when you couldn't afford it. You don't know what you're talking about. Don't act like you can relate."

Aunt June's face grew pale. She sat there silent, looking at Mama sadly. "Maybe you're right. I don't know what all that's like. And you'll never know how much that hurts me every day, knowing I missed out on something so wonderful." Her voice shook. "But I do know one thing. You have such good kids here. They love you, and they need you. I'm sorry about George. Maybe there's nothing you can do for him anymore, I don't know." She shrugged. "But what about the rest of them? Your girls need you right now. They *need* their Mama." Aunt June stood up. She picked the crumbled muffin off the ground.

The wooden stairs hurt Caroline's bony bottom. She straightened her back and moved her head, but now the door blocked Aunt June.

"I just hope you don't realize that when it's too late," Aunt June said.

Mama put her head in her hands and leaned against the table, as if she had a bad headache and wanted to block out any noise.

Aunt June took the papers with her and made her way to the front door.

"Oh, no," Phoebe said, jumping up.

Caroline stood up too, but, too late. Aunt June was already at the door.

She had tears in her eyes. She wiped them away and tried to throw on a smile.

"Hello, girls, I brought muffins."

Phoebe grabbed Aunt June's arm. "What's wrong with Mama?"

The smile disappeared. "Y'all heard that, huh?"

Caroline nodded.

Aunt June sighed. "Instead of me staying for dinner, what do you say you spend the night at my place?"

"Stay over? Oh, good!" Phoebe ran up the stairs to pack an overnight sack. It was too good to be true for her to get to go to two places in one day after being stuck inside so much.

"I wish you could be excited like that," Aunt June said to Caroline with a sigh. "But you always know when something's not right these days."

Caroline nodded. She did know almost everything, which was good and bad. It was easier not to understand what was going on sometimes, easier to be young like Phoebe.

She glanced at the papers in Aunt June's hand. Even turned upside down, she recognized the tiny handwriting through the paper.

Mama had been reading George's letters again.

Chapter 11

"Do I really have to go?" Caroline sat at the edge of the bed, gripping the mattress until her knuckles turned white. Surely Aunt June would understand. She wasn't old and cranky like Aunt Elsmere. She wouldn't make her do something she didn't want to.

Aunt June finished the braid in Phoebe's hair with a little green bow to match her dress. She tilted her own head of curly red hair and looked at Caroline real hard. "I'm sorry, but, yes, you must."

Caroline felt her eyes grow big. "But Miss Evelyn's house is nasty. She's got trash everywhere. Besides, no one will know. Miss Evelyn doesn't go to church, and we haven't been since the day Aunt Elsmere said I'd help there. No one has to know if I miss."

Aunt June put her hands on her hips. "Now *you'd* know. And Miss Evelyn would know. God would know."

That was supposed to make Caroline feel bad, but she didn't. Only one week into June, and it was extra hot that day. They were really only entering the worst of the heat, though. July and August would be miserable. Working in that smelly house would be unbearable.

Aunt June sighed. She always seemed to know what Caroline was thinking. "I'm sorry, hun, but you're committed. When you commit to something, even if it's something you don't want to do, you need to stick with it. I know how dirty Miss Evelyn's house is. But she's an old lady. She's probably looking forward to your visit."

Caroline didn't walk Phoebe home on her way to Miss Evelyn's. Aunt June said they would stay until suppertime, and Phoebe didn't want to go home. Caroline didn't say so, but she didn't want to either, after the mean way Mama had spoken to

Aunt June. And Mama wouldn't mind. She probably hadn't even noticed they weren't there last night.

Hardly a body was outside on such a blistering day. People who could spare time from their work escaped to places in town, or stayed inside the shadiest part of their home with a bucket of ice. It was just too hot to do much of anything. What Caroline would give to sneak into the movies instead of going to Miss Evelyn's!

But Robert wasn't lucky to be working at the theater that day either. He was the only person Caroline passed on her way to Miss Evelyn's.

"Hey, Caroline," he said, tipping his hat to her, the way he always did.

"Hi there."

Robert stopped walking. He fanned his face with the hat. Its rim was almost dripping in the sunlight. "Listen, have you seen Blanche today? I've come by several times the last few days, and she's always gone."

"Well, she was at Elsa Mae's yesterday. Why don't you try there?"

Robert's hand paused in midair. "That's what she told you? I asked Elsa Mae earlier, and she hasn't seen her since last week."

"Well, that's all she said. Maybe Elsa Mae wasn't home, so she went somewhere else. Maybe she's at Thomas's visitin' Pamelia. She goes there a lot, too." And never helps with a blasted thing, she wanted to add, but stopped herself. It wouldn't do any good to scare off the person Blanche would marry.

Robert's eyes darted back and forth, thinking, puzzled. "Maybe. Yeah, maybe so. I'll try that, kiddo. Thanks."

But the doubt in his voice spoke stronger than his words.

Caroline turned and watched him disappear around the bend in the road. Robert mustn't have known about Blanche riding in the car that one night. Unless Elsa Mae bought a car and learned how to drive, Blanche was probably sneaking off with someone. But maybe she'd gone with Betty and that person who'd driven them to the Bisbee Show. Maybe she'd just gotten a ride home and had forgotten to mention it.

Again, though, the doubt spoke stronger.

Miss Evelyn had a nice, large blue jay shot in its left eye and waiting dead on the front porch when Caroline arrived.

"Look what I caught in my tomato garden today." Miss Evelyn picked it up with her bare hands, proud of herself. She smiled and revealed her dirty teeth.

Caroline's stomach turned. Was it too late to run away?

Miss Evelyn put the bird in a paper sack. "Let's come on inside a minute," she said. Thankfully she at least washed her hands at the kitchen sink.

"What do you need me to do today, Miss Evelyn?" Caroline leaned against the counter. Hopefully she'd get to do something outside and stay busy and the time would fly. She'd shown up early so she'd get done fast.

Miss Evelyn handed her a large bowl of peas. "You can just sit on the porch and shell these for me."

Shelling peas was boring, no matter how someone looked at it. There was just no way around it. But, somehow, like it had been during the rainstorm, there was a surprisingly odd peacefulness about being there, sitting in the shade. Miss Evelyn sat in her rocker, not bothering Caroline or saying a word to her. Once more, no one was nagging at her. She was doing something, yet it didn't take much concentration. Her fingers worked mechanically, splitting the green outer shells around the peas, scooping the peas out with her fingertips, coated in slime, and putting them in a bowl. There was a separate bowl for the pods that looked too thin. These were young and not ready.

The peas hit the bowl rhythmically, multiplying, while the bowl of pods grew smaller.

The orange cat came from the yard and jumped up in Miss Evelyn's lap. How strange that these cats loved her when she acted so cruel to any unlucky animal she caught in that tomato garden! Miss Evelyn rubbed the cat behind the ears and on its belly. It purred loudly.

"My friend, Peter, just had a new litter of kittens." Caroline emptied some more peas into the bowl. "He's letting me take one when it gets a little bit bigger."

Miss Evelyn nodded. "It's never a good thing to take something away from its mama too soon."

Caroline cracked another shell open. "Maybe it will come with me one of these Wednesdays."

Miss Evelyn smiled. "I'd like that."

"Is there anything else you'd like me to do?" Caroline set the large bowl of peas on the kitchen table, along with the smaller bowl of pods not ready to be shelled.

"Well, I really enjoyed you reading last time."

"You did? I thought you'd fallen asleep."

Miss Evelyn gave her a sharp look. "Why I did eventually, yes. But when someone's reading to me, I like to close my eyes and imagine it."

Uh-oh. How long had it been before she'd fallen asleep last time? Did she know Caroline had snooped?

Miss Evelyn handed her the Bible.

Caroline took the book and started turning on a lamp.

"No!" Miss Evelyn waved her hand as if she was shooing a fly away.

"But it's not raining. You won't get electrocuted today."

"But that electric is expensive. It's a waste."

"Well, not trying to be rude, but why do you have it?"

"Girl, you look here." Miss Evelyn frowned. "That *is* rude, and it ain't none of your business." She started to go back outside. "But since you asked, I ain't never wanted it. My son, Harry, got it for me."

Caroline's ears perked up. Harry was a name in that letter. So Miss Evelyn definitely was the recipient. Was she also the one in that photo?

Caroline sat back down on her chair on the porch, but she didn't open the Bible.

"How many children do you have?"

"Aren't you full of questions today?" Miss Evelyn grunted. "Two. A girl and a boy. They'd done grown and left me. They think paying for electric will erase the fact they never come to see me."

Caroline swallowed. "I'm sorry."

Miss Evelyn shrugged. She picked up another cat, a brown one. "Don't be. Ain't your fault. Now turn to the book of Ruth."

Phoebe held onto her rag doll with one hand and grabbed the end of the blanket with the other. Caroline helped her spread the checkered blanket evenly over the Rock. Then they climbed on top of it, perching the lantern on the end in front of them. Even in the darkness, the Rock still felt warm from all the sun it soaked up during the day. The heat found its way through the blanket and to their bare legs and toes. Caroline shifted into a comfortable position on her side.

"Is this just like you used to do it?" Phoebe asked, squeezing her doll to her chest.

Poor Phoebe. Always wondering about how things used to be, before George had gone, before things seemed so much harder.

"Yes," Caroline said, though it wasn't exactly. It used to be four of them sitting out under the stars, and lots of times

Mama and Papa and Aunt June. "George used to love sitting out here every night in the summertime."

"I remember we did last year, when I was six." Phoebe picked up the large glass of lemonade they'd brought and took a sip.

"Yeah, we did." The crickets chirped, the air was hot, and everything looked the same. But nothing felt the same.

"Tell me a story."

Caroline took the glass and swallowed a large mouthful. The lemonade had gotten warm, but it was sweet and sour against her dry tongue. She took another drink. "Well, let's see. The fairies only come out during the summertime. The rest of the year, they sleep underneath the Rock. Waayyyy down under there. But during the summer, when they come up from hibernating, when they have their babies, that's when the Rock grows. And it's our growing season too."

"What do you mean?" Phoebe's eyes got wide.

What was it George used to say? Something about growing up. "Well—uh—you see, the fairies are what make us grow, too. They come out at night and whisper sweet thoughts in our ears when we're sleeping. That's what makes us have sweet dreams. That's what makes us grow. It worked on Pamelia. She just started expecting during the summer, so that means the fairies gave her a baby."

Phoebe stared at her as if she didn't quite believe it. "What about when we have bad dreams?"

"Well, that means we're growing an awful lot at once. Like a growth spurt. And so we don't have time to stop and enjoy the dream. It gets jumbled up and ends up bad."

Phoebe paused. She took a sip of lemonade. "But what about the rest of the year?"

"Oh, the fairies leave enough fairy dust floating around to help us grow all year. We just grow up the most during the summer."

Phoebe nodded, her face serious. "Do you think I'm

growing? Do you think I'll be ready to do school?"

Phoebe looked almost smaller now than she had when she was five. She was taller, but her collar bone stuck out so sharp, from her low weight, it was hard to look at sometimes. Her head seemed too big for her tiny frame. What could Caroline say? That they may not get to start school if Papa wasn't back and they had to do all of the work to manage the farm? That didn't seem fair.

Phoebe's blue eyes twinkled under the stars.

"Of course you will. But we need to make sure we get enough sleep so we grow." Caroline grabbed her hand and jumped off the rock. "I'll race you to the porch."

She gave Phoebe a head start.

"Caroline?"

Caroline rolled over on the cot. Her face felt sticky from sweating in her sleep.

"Caroline?"

Something shook her shoulder. Why was a thick blanket on top of her? No wonder it was so hot. Caroline sat up.

The sky just barely had a soft glow in the distance. Phoebe had the blanket pulled up to her chin. "Caroline, I don't feel good."

Caroline felt wide awake now. Her heart pounded. "What is it?" Even in the early morning light, it was easy to see that Phoebe looked pale and clammy.

"I feel bad."

"I'm going to get Aunt Elsmere." Caroline lit the lantern and fled inside the house.

Phoebe's fever had returned.

Chapter 12

The onions burned Caroline's eyes. It felt as if the heat from the sun had finally found its way into her eyes, stinging them and causing tears to run down her cheeks. But she refused to stop. She kept slicing one onion after the other.

There was little she could do. There was little any of them could do. But standing there, chopping the onions for the soup that was supposed to help Phoebe made it feel as if she was doing something, but it didn't feel like enough. If she could only take some of the pain that Phoebe, so small and young, felt, she gladly would. She'd take all of it.

Phoebe hadn't yet been out of bed and somewhat back to normal for even a week when her fever returned. No one else ever caught any of Phoebe's illnesses. The doctor said it was because she'd been born sick, and the pneumonia had weakened her even more.

What would become of her? Would she suffer like this and get better, only to keep getting sick again? Would she be like Beth in *Little Women*? The sweet, unselfish one of the family who sometimes got taken for granted? Was it wrong to tell her stories and get her hopes up about going to school? Was it silly to wish that maybe she really would go?

Caroline sliced a piece of onion with a force that missed and punctured her finger. She tossed the knife down on the cutting board and cleaned the cut with a wet rag. Tears still streamed down her face. The kitchen felt even more suffocating than normal. Liquid dripped down her chest all the way to the tops of her legs.

More tears fell—not from the onions, but from the thought of losing Phoebe, Phoebe "so sweet, and yet so feeble," as Papa had once said.

If the day ever came, would she be strong enough? No, Caroline wasn't. She wasn't strong enough to say goodbye.

"Where have you *been*?"

Blanche looked at Caroline as if she'd just been slapped in the face.

"Why does it matter?"

"Because I can't do everything on my own, that's why."

Blanche shrugged. She bit into an apple. "Seems to me you can. Papa thought so anyway, the way he always talked about you."

"It's not fair to drag Papa into this. I had to do all the inside chores myself while Aunt Elsmere took care of Phoebe. None of the outside chores have been done yet. So why won't you tell me *where* you've been? You're always gone." Caroline wiped her greasy hands on her apron.

"I was seeing Elsa Mae—"

"Have you now? Because I know you've lied at least once. And what about your own family? Why can't you help here? This isn't fair, and you know it." Caroline felt herself shout the words, and she clenched her fists. "Have you talked to Robert any?"

"Don't you go around talking about things you don't understand." Blanche's voice shook. She threw her unfinished apple on the kitchen counter and stormed up the stairs.

That next week was one of the hardest Caroline had ever faced. Mama hardly came out of her room. Aunt Elsmere spent all of her time with Phoebe, who kept coughing and having fever.

Doctor Reynolds came several times and said she had developed another form of pneumonia.

Her lungs and entire body were already so weak from before, that it was all they could do to break the fever and get her strong enough to sit up and eat.

Peter came by and tended to their crops, but Caroline only got a couple of words with him here and there. Aunt June and Uncle P. Joe stopped by all the time and brought food or oversaw the tiny bit of hired help they were behind on paying. One day there seemed to be more colored people than usual working, and Caroline knew that Uncle P. Joe had paid more people to work. She also knew he'd never tell Papa, so Papa would never repay him.

Blanche still disappeared during the day and often at night, but now she didn't talk to Caroline at all. She didn't even bother using the drainage pipe anymore. She just went when she pleased, and no one else bothered to ask.

The one time Aunt Elsmere asked if she was going to see Robert, Blanche shrugged at his name and muttered something about going to the post office. Had Blanche already reached a level of boredom she eventually developed with all the men she dated?

It was no wonder that Caroline began to look forward to going to Miss Evelyn's. It was an escape from the sickness and Mama's never-ending sadness. And since she couldn't get away from Ripley, getting out of her own home was better than nothing.

"I know how you feel," Miss Evelyn said one day. "A body can only handle so much."

Caroline didn't say anything. If she sat there quietly and wound Miss Evelyn's yarn ball for her, maybe the old lady would open up and tell her story.

Eventually, she did.

"My husband—" Miss Evelyn's voice shook.

"It's okay. You don't have to—"

"Just listen," Miss Evelyn said with a snap. Her tone softened. "My husband beat me. Not at first, but a few years into our marriage. He hurt me bad. He drank. Drank an awful lot, and then he'd change and he'd hurt me. No one knew, not even the children. The only one who did was my sister."

Gertrude. The lady who wrote that letter.

"I was in my early twenties when it started. We lived in the north. My family had lots of money. John, he had lots of money, too, but he drank most of it away. Finally, I decided I couldn't do it anymore." Miss Evelyn rubbed one of her cats with a wrinkled hand. "I took the children and we left him one night. We went far, far away. Down here to the south. I told people my husband had died. It wasn't too long after that that I learned he *did* die. He drank too much."

Caroline's breath caught in her throat. Miss Evelyn sat there in that rocking chair, a confused, lonely, old lady. One minute she told Caroline something personal like that, the next, she was shooting at things or fussing about not needing any help.

What was it like to hurt that bad that you were confused so much? Caroline knew how awful it was for someone you loved to leave you. But what was it like when you had to be the one doing the leaving?

Another letter from Papa had arrived at the post office. Thomas brought it when he came to chop cotton.

"Here ya go, Mama," he said, patting her thin shoulder. Mama sat on the bed next to Phoebe. Caroline and Aunt Elsmere sat on chairs beside the bed. Blanche was nowhere to be found.

Mama's eyes brightened. Some of the shadows lifted from her face, and for a moment she looked like Mama again.

"Thank you, Thomas," she managed and squeezed his large, tanned hand with her thin, pale one, so thin you could see the blue, little veins poking up. "Would you please read it?"

"Of course." Thomas opened the envelope and sat at the edge of the bed so Caroline could see it too. It didn't matter if someone read out loud, she liked to read along and see it, word for word, on her own.

"*Dear my darling 'Little Women,'*" Thomas began. He grinned at Caroline. Even he knew about her favorite book. "*I'm so sorry I haven't been able to write. It ain't really that I wasn't able to but that there hasn't been much to write about. I'm still working at this 5 to 5 store. The Brewer family is real nice and pays me on time like he said he would. I'm mainly helping em with figures and the accounts families have set up. When I'm not doing that, I'm restless, and I unpack shipments and sweep the floors. It's so different from what I've always done. I definitely prefer the country life over being in a city. This ain't even a city, just a slightly bigger town than Ripley. It's a city enough for me, though.*

I have enough saved for a set of mules already, but I'm holding out to get us more horses too. I want to have extra money just for emergencies. June called and said Phoebe was sick. I wondered if something was wrong cause I hadn't heard back. Here's money to help with that. I hope that can cover any doctor visits and medicine she may need. How bad is it? Is she feelin better? If I need to come home, please let me know as quickly as you can.

I put in extra money for Blanche to set aside for her wedding. I know it means a lot to her, so it's not much, but it's something, maybe enough for a new dress.

I love all of you so much, and I miss you more than you'll know. Please take care."

Thomas set the letter down on his lap. "*Love always, Papa.*" His voice trailed off.

All of them were silent for several minutes. Were they also wondering if Papa needed to come home? Phoebe hadn't said a word all morning. She'd grown thinner than ever, her hair hung flat against her head, and she lay under the covers, freezing even though Miss Evelyn's thermometer had read ninety-eight degrees.

The bed felt strange with just her in it. It seemed too big for one person. Caroline kicked the sheet away from her. She rolled over on her side and pulled her nightgown up so that her legs were bare. The sheets felt damp underneath her. They stuck to her skin just like her nightgown.

Finally, the door opened. Blanche walked in. She didn't light a candle, or undress like normal. She just stood there with her arms wrapped around herself, her little, red hat dangling from her fingers. She stared straight ahead, not really seeing Caroline in the dark. What was she looking at? Was something wrong? What time was it?

"Blanche?" Caroline sat up. The damp sheets felt cool all of a sudden. "Are you all right?"

Blanche still held her hat. She moved close and sat on the end of the bed.

"I don't know," she whispered.

"What do you mean you don't know? How can you not know? You're all right, or you're not."

Blanche sighed. "I mean—I don't know, exactly. I'm nervous I guess."

"About what? About Phoebe?"

"That too." Her voice sounded a bit shaky. "Just seems like things have changed awful fast."

Caroline nodded. They sure were different lately.

"And—I guess I feel a little unsure."

"About—?" That was a first. When had Blanche ever felt unsure about anything? She was so confident and always knew what she wanted, or what she needed to do.

"About getting married."

That was also a first. Blanche's wedding was all she ever used to talk about.

"Everyone gets a little nervous. That's normal. Aunt June told me that once. You'll be fine. That letter from Papa sounds like he'll be home real soon. I'm sure once he's back, you'll get to marry Robert. He even sent money so you can buy a dress."

Blanche fidgeted with the hat and tossed it on the floor. She trembled now. "That's just it, Caroline. I won't get married when Papa comes home."

What was she saying? Had she and Robert argued?

"Of course you will." Caroline petted Blanche on the shoulder. "Of course you will. Everyone has their fights. Mama and Papa have argued before. That doesn't mean they don't love each other."

Blanche stared out the window into the moonlight. "I won't get married when he's home. I can't," she whispered. "Because I'm already married."

Caroline's hand stopped moving. "Wh—when did you get married? Did you get sick of waiting?"

Blanche didn't answer for a minute. "Something like that," she said slowly.

"It's okay. Mama and Papa won't be mad." If anything, that was one less thing for Papa to worry about. No need to spend money they didn't have on a wedding now. "Why Aunt June eloped when she was sixteen! They'll all understand. You don't have to feel bad if there's no big wedding."

Blanche still didn't say anything.

"Blanche?" Caroline let go of Blanche's shoulder and moved back to her place. "You can still have a party and invite everyone."

Finally Blanche looked at her. The light from the window shone on only the right side of her face.

"I got married last week—but not to Robert."

Caroline sat there and didn't say anything. Her hand lay motionless on Blanche's shoulder. Had it been so obvious? Certainly, the signs had been there all along. Was Caroline too young to recognize anything for what it was, or had she just not wanted to see what was happening?

Or was it that Blanche was plain good at changing her mind and hiding things from people?

Maybe it had been a combination of lots of things.

Blanche buried her face in Caroline's lap for the longest time, letting her sobs hide in the soft, thin nightgown.

A lump rose in Caroline's throat. How could this be? That someone could be so unhappy at the time everyone claimed was supposed to be the best in a girl's life? Blanche, who had been looking at wedding dresses in Mama's catalogs ever since she'd been Caroline's age?

Was this new husband a bad person? Was he like Miss Evelyn's old husband?

"Blanche. Blanche, please answer this question." Caroline took a deep breath. She rubbed the top of Blanche's head, the hair all tangled from lying down. "What's wrong? Is he—has he—does he ever—hurt you?"

Blanche sat up. Her eyes widened. "No, no, never. Kenneth—I don't know if you ever even met him. He's Robert's friend who drove us to the Bisbee show that night— he's just wonderful. I mean, really the best person I've ever met. We belong together. I thought I loved Robert, but I don't. He's just too dull and poor and drinks too much, and it's just—I can't spend the rest of my life with someone I don't really love."

Those words stabbed Caroline with pain. *Don't really love.* Robert *had* really loved Blanche—that was sure. All those years of trying to get her attention, months of forgiving her for silly things, days of working at the theater, only to work in the fields afterwards so he could provide for her—slipped away into nothing.

Did he know yet? Was that why Blanche cried? Did she feel bad?

If she didn't feel bad, she needed to. Part of Caroline wanted to shake Blanche for throwing away something so important. But what good would it do?

"Well, then, I'm sure it's for the best, if you didn't love him—the way he loved you."

Blanche started sobbing again. Uncontrollable, loud sobs. Caroline handed her a handkerchief and rubbed her arm to try to get her to quiet down. If Aunt Elsmere didn't know, this wasn't a good way to find out.

"Blanche, calm down. No one will be mad if you did what's best for you. If Kenneth's a good person like you say, then maybe it's better this way."

"You don't understand." Blanche hiccupped. Her whole body shook. "You just don't understand."

"*What* don't I understand?"

"No one's gonna be happy about this. Especially Aunt Elsmere." Blanche put her head back in Caroline's lap, as if she couldn't finish and look her in the face at the same time.

"You mean she'll be mad she didn't get to come to the wedding, or that you married someone else? Somebody she didn't know?"

"She'll be upset we *had* to get married. I would've called off the engagement with Robert the proper way and waited a while, till Papa comes home. But it couldn't wait." The sobs slowed down a bit. Blanche's voice had grown to a whisper. "We *had* to get married."

Caroline's hand froze again. Her breath felt as if it had been knocked out of her. It all made sense now.

Thomas and Pamelia weren't the only ones expecting.

Chapter 13

"*Why do I always have to be the boy?*" Caroline put her hands on her hips. Papa's pair of Sunday trousers almost slid off her slim waist, even with rope tied around the top to hold them up. It was hot, and the pants made everything a lot hotter.

"*Cause I'm older, and I want to be the bride. Besides, this dress fits me better.*" Blanche pushed her chest out slightly. Even at the age of eleven, she had a good figure forming. Mama's old yellow dress she'd worn when she was a teenager was a little too long on her, but otherwise it fit okay. Another year and it would fit just fine.

"*It's not fair!*" Caroline kicked her feet and sat down on the sofa. Every time they played wedding, she got stuck being the groom.

"*Shush, you two,*" Thomas said from the corner of the room. "*Ya'll are so loud, I can hardly hear the radio. If you don't keep it down, you'll wake up Ma.*"

Blanche gently smoothed out the skirt of her dress. She put some gloves over her hands and picked up the flowers from the end table. She went in the kitchen where Mama kept her purse hanging on a knob in the corner and put a coat of red lipstick on.

It was pouring outside. Even in the kitchen, with all the window shades open, it was nearly dark. Everything smelled damp and musty.

"*I want some lipstick too,*" Caroline said, reaching for the shiny, little tube.

"*Boys don't wear lipstick,*" Blanche laughed. "*Now let's finish the game. Let's practice walking down the aisle.*"

"*I'm not a boy!*"

"*Just pretend.*"

"*Shut up!*" Thomas growled. He leaned closer to the radio so he wouldn't miss anything. Something about his favorite ball player, Babe Ruth.

Caroline yanked off the pants and threw them on the floor. Who cared if they got wrinkled? It would be Blanche's fault because she was older. She was the one who made them put on the nice clothes that weren't theirs.

"Pick those up, Caroline," Blanche said with her teeth clenched the way she did whenever she got really angry.

"No. I don't have to. I ain't gonna." Caroline started walking away, but where could she go in such a tiny house? Mama was big and expecting and she couldn't go bother her. Mama had said not to go outside until the storm passed. Papa was still gone taking crops into town. He probably got stuck staying at Aunt June's on the way back.

She began going to her room, but it would be only minutes before Blanche would come in and continue arguing. Blanche and her stupid wedding game. There were lots of other things they could've played, and she had to choose that.

George's head suddenly appeared out of the ceiling, upside down. The large, black aviator goggles Mama had ordered from the Sears catalog for his Christmas stocking covered half his face.

"Who goes there?"

Caroline giggled. "Me."

" 'Me' is an odd name. Where are you traveling to?"

Caroline thought a moment. Anywhere away from Blanche would be good. "Anywhere, I guess."

"Anywhere can be right here. You have to be specific when you're flying a plane. You even gotta know longitude and latitude."

"What's that?"

George's face was bright pink from all the blood that had rushed to his head. He moaned and pulled himself up. He disappeared a second. Then the ladder to the attic flew down. "All aboard, ma'am."

Caroline climbed the ladder as fast as she could before Blanche came up.

George pulled the ladder back up and shut the door. It was weird being in the small attic. They never went up there except maybe during the fall and winter to get things down. But it wasn't that hot because the round window that overlooked the cotton fields was open. The wind blew in the opposite direction, so the rain hardly got inside.

George crawled in front of the window and grabbed a barrel lid. He turned it as if it was a steering wheel. Maps and books lay sprawled out before him.

"Testing, testing, one, two, three. It's going to be a bumpy landing."

Caroline sat next to him. A few drops of rain sprinkled on her knees, and she shivered. The land seemed endless from up here. In the rain, the cotton fields looked like the sea, or at least what she thought the sea probably looked like. She'd never seen the ocean. Least not outside of pictures. She'd seen the Mississippi River, though.

"Do rivers and oceans look the same?"

"No time for talk. We have to care for the passengers." George handed her a telescope. "Let me know when you see land."

"Do I have to be a boy?"

George snapped out of the game for a moment. "Why would you have to be a boy?"

"Well, I don't know. Can girls fly planes?"

George laughed. "Didn't you see Papa's paper the other day?

Caroline rolled her eyes. She couldn't read on her own yet.

"Well, that lady, Amy Johnson, flew eleven thousand miles by herself. All the way from England to Australia. Sure girls can fly." He turned on his pilot voice again. "It's a new age we're livin' in, kiddo. You can do anything."

He turned his wheel to the left and right, swinging his body sideways, bumping into Caroline.

Caroline closed her eyes a minute. The wind blew her hair from her face.

"I repeat. It's going to be a bumpy landing. Grab the parachutes and get ready!"

Caroline groaned and picked up her pile of books. So much for a short escape plan from everyone arguing. It was so warm up in the attic that black spots danced in front of her when she moved. She now had to duck when she stood next to the window that had once been George's pilot seat. She opened the attic door and let down the ladder.

She climbed down the narrow ladder, tucking her dress up in between her legs. She held her books underneath her left armpit.

Blanche and Aunt Elsmere were still in the sitting room, yelling back and forth.

"It doesn't matter what you think," Blanche snapped. "I'm a married *woman* now."

"Married to a man who wasn't ever your fiancé. What will people think? What will people say?"

Caroline shoved the ladder back into the ceiling. She stood at the top of the stairs, fanning herself with the Amelia Earhart book Aunt June loaned her.

"Who cares what anyone thinks!" Blanche slammed something down on the table.

"Well, I do."

"Well, you don't care *that* much. If you did, maybe you wouldn't be living in your sister's home driving everyone nuts."

Everything grew quiet.

"Damn you." The door slammed. Everything got quiet again.

Blanche started walking toward the stairs. Caroline ran into the bedroom. She sat by the window and opened the book, as if she'd been reading the whole time and not standing in the hallway listening.

Blanche walked in, tears streaming down her angry face.

"I've never, ever heard her curse before." She flopped down on the bed, staring up at the ceiling.

Caroline nodded. Probably not many people had. She sighed and closed the book. She moved to the bed and let Blanche put her head in her lap once more. She rocked her back and forth like she did with Phoebe, and for a long time, Blanche's crying was the only sound in the room.

"I guess I need to start packing," Blanche said finally. She stumbled from the bed and began pulling her clothes from the chifferobe.

"Blanche, do you—do you need any help?"

Blanche broke into tears. She walked over to Caroline and hugged her. "Oh, Caroline. You're always so good to everyone. Even when they don't deserve it."

Caroline shrugged and picked up one of the sweaters Blanche had dropped and refolded it. If Blanche had known the mean things Caroline had thought so many times before, she wouldn't say that.

"So, what are you going to do? Where are you and Kenneth moving?" It felt strange no longer saying Robert's name— Robert, who they'd known for years—and instead mentioning a fellow Caroline only remembered vaguely from the Bisbee Show. A person who meant nothing more than a pair of headlights on a summer night.

Blanche dropped some of her things into a brown, paper sack. "I don't know, exactly. I think we're going to Arkansas to be with his family. You know, before I start showing." Blanche gulped. "We'll go in a few days if we can."

A few days? Would they even wait for Phoebe to get better? Or for Mama to act normal again? Was she going to write Papa?

"I know what you're thinking," Blanche said. "But, please, just don't tell me." Her eyes filled up. "Just please don't tell me how stupid I am. I need you on my side."

Caroline pulled some of the clothes out of the sack and distributed them into another separate one. Blanche did a lot of stupid things. Like cramming everything into one flimsy sack that'd break from being so full. Or running off all the time. Or getting pregnant.

But seeing her so weak made Caroline feel sorry for her.

"You're not stupid." She put her hand on her shoulder. "I don't understand it at all." She sighed. "I just wish I'd known. All this time, since the Bisbee Show, you've liked Kenneth, and I didn't know."

Blanche looked at the floor. "I mentioned it that night."

That comment. About the car. It made sense now. Why hadn't Caroline remembered it? "I miss how close we used to be. Like how I am with Phoebe now."

Blanche smiled through her tears. "I was never nice to you all the time the way you are with Phoebe."

Caroline shrugged. "But I was never sick all the time like Phoebe either." Caroline put her head against Blanche's shoulder. "I just can't believe you made me do all the wedding practicing and pretending to be a boy for nothing."

Blanche laughed weakly. "Well, Amy had to dress up as a boy in that book of yours. Guess I thought you wouldn't mind."

"Nice try. That's long before I could read!"

Blanche wiped her face again and got quiet.

Caroline was afraid to ask the most important question. When was Blanche going to tell Mama everything? And what exactly was she going to tell her?

For two miserable days, Caroline helped Aunt Elsmere take care of Phoebe. She didn't spend any time working outside anymore. There was no point when both Mama and Phoebe seemed to need her so much. And there was too much work and now not enough people to get anything done. Thomas and Uncle P. Joe came to check on everything when they could, but the cotton crop was probably just going to be a very poor one that year.

Blanche hardly dared to show her face at home. She left before any of them were awake and came home after dark.

"Doesn't bother me one bit. Silly girl. Shouldn't be living here or eating any of our food at all since she's got a man to care for her." Aunt Elsmere grunted, sloshing more of the soup into a bowl to bring to Phoebe. "Guess he ain't much of a man, though, if he can't provide. If he has to go running home to his mama and dump his mistakes and shame on his family."

Caroline put the lid on the hot pot of soup when Aunt Elsmere walked away. Her shoulders ached. Not from working, because she lately hadn't done the hard kind of work she was used to, but from the worry of hovering over Phoebe and Mama and from restless sleep. She wiped her hands on her apron and sat at the kitchen table.

Mama was almost as bad as Phoebe lately. She looked so thin, and all she did was sleep. When she talked, it seemed mechanical, as if she didn't really hear or understand what they were talking about. Her eyes stared into space, looking at something Caroline couldn't see.

Aunt Elsmere had at last gotten her way and won her argument with Mama about where Phoebe slept. She'd moved Phoebe into Thomas and George's old room, which already seemed much better. Phoebe needed to be by herself, away from Mama. She needed space both to be ill and to recover.

Mama didn't seem to notice.

Caroline picked up an apple and bit into it. The sweet tartness startled her dry tongue. It was the first food she'd eaten since the day before, and it was odd to realize that. Maybe shutting things off the way Mama did wasn't so difficult, after all.

What would Papa say if he could see his "little women" now?

"You need to at least tell your mother that you're married," Aunt Elsmere fussed in a low tone. "Even if you don't want to tell her the rest of it."

Dishes clattered. Blanche must've been drying them.

Caroline felt Aunt June stiffen beside her. She stopped moving the swing. A door slammed. It sounded as if someone was stomping up the stairs.

"Here we go again." Caroline sighed.

"Has it been that bad?" Aunt June began moving the swing with her feet again.

"Every time Aunt Elsmere sees Blanche, or thinks about her, she goes crazy."

Aunt June sighed. "She's just worried for her. Blanche has made some choices that've put her in a tough spot. How in the world does your mama still not know anything, though?"

Caroline shrugged. "Neither is saying much out loud where Mama can hear it. And you know Aunt Elmere doesn't want Phoebe to know anything. Aunt Elsmere said telling Mama is Blanche's job and no one else's."

"Oh, dear. I'm sure your mama thinks it's you and Blanche arguing like usual. Who knows how much she even has heard. She's been asleep every time I drop by."

A lightning bug landed on Caroline's knee. She put her hand over it and watched it glow between her fingers.

When George had lived there, he always did things to get them in trouble. But whenever he did, he had somehow known exactly the right words to say to make it better.

Too bad George wasn't there.

Caroline opened her hand and watched the lightning bug fly away.

The next morning, Blanche came out of Mama's room. Her face was pale, and she had a shawl wrapped around her shoulders.

"Oh, no, Blanche, you're not sick, are you?"

Blanche wrapped her arms around her stomach. It still looked so tiny and perfect. Would it really grow round the way she heard Pamelia's was?

"I feel so queasy. Every day for the past couple of weeks, I've been throwing up awful. It's worse than the cramping."

Caroline didn't say anything. It all sounded horrible. She'd rather stay small the way she was and never have to go through any of it. She'd rather not date or marry anyone if this was what it could lead to. She helped Blanche sit down on the top step.

Blanche pulled her shawl off, now hot, and fanned her face. "Will you help me finish packing? We're leaving tomorrow morning."

"So soon? Am I at least gonna get to meet this man?"

"We need to leave as soon as possible. His family doesn't know much yet. Just that he's married."

Blanche held her stomach again. "And, no, Aunt Elsmere doesn't want him coming anywhere near here."

Caroline held Blanche's hand. She had done something no one liked. She had acted in a way that had changed everything. But how many times had she messed up and been forgiven before? After all, she was still part of the family. She was still Blanche.

Caroline squeezed her hand. "Well, when you're ready, I'd like to meet him. I want to know my brother-in-law."

Blanche gave a weak smile. "I knew you would." After a minute, the color returned to her face.

"What did you tell Mama?"

"Everything."

"Well, what did she say?"

Blanche shrugged. "Nothing. Not a word. She just rolled over."

Chapter 14

Caroline kicked the gravel in the road and didn't look back.

Peter was way behind her, calling her name. He was running toward her, wearing his old pants and thin, white shirt. He was headed toward the water hole. He always wore those old clothes when he went swimming.

So what? She didn't have to answer. *She* was on her way to help an elderly lady. What was he doing? Swimming. Skipping chores, probably. Nothing as important. He hadn't come by to help her in over a week. He'd missed all the Blanche drama. It wasn't as if he were busy helping his own family either. He wasn't. At least not all the time.

Not when he walked by with that girl Anna who used to sit in front of Caroline every day last year. Where'd they'd been? To the movies? To the water hole? Was he meeting her there now?

Peter's steps grew closer. "Hey, I've been calling you. Do you wanna come play ball with us tonight?"

Caroline kept walking.

"Hey, wait up," he said.

She slowed down a bit.

"I said, do you wanna come play ball tonight?" Peter wiped his forehead with his shirt tail. The shirt seemed smaller than it had before, and his arms looked bigger. "Some of us are gonna meet up at sunset and play. Light as it was last night with the moon and stars, I reckon we'll see real good. Bunch of kids from school are comin'. My mom's making her sweet tea for us. Then some of the guys and I may sneak to up to the Sugar Hill mansion just to poke around and have some fun."

Caroline clenched her books. So here Peter was, not talking to her or coming to check on them for the last few days, wanting to play baseball? He'd invited "a bunch of kids from school." That probably meant Anna. Why would she want to tag along like a little kid while they flirted? Was this why he'd acted odd around her when she had last spent time with him? Maybe he'd been trying to make his mind up between both of them. Clearly, he'd made it up.

"What's wrong? Want to come swim? I'm headed there now."

"No, I can't. I'm going to Miss Evelyn's." There, she'd made up her mind, too.

"Ah, shucks." Peter kicked a rock in the road. "Why are you going on a Tuesday? Thought Wednesday was your day? Just skip it."

Caroline stopped. When would he grow up? "Maybe if you got to know her, you'd like her." Her voice rose. "I go all the time, whenever I please. It feels good to help someone else. Not like you'd know." She started walking again, only faster than before.

"What's that supposed to mean?"

Caroline rolled her eyes. She had to tell him everything, otherwise he would never get it. "Nothing. Just that here you are swimming and having fun, while I've been stuck inside cleaning and caring for a sick person and listening to people argue. No telling what Aunt June has spent on the helping hands, since no one would help us. My mama's acting like a vegetable, sitting there, just withering away into nothing. While your mama's wasting time making sweet tea and you're walking around flirting with every girl who comes along and getting her hopes up, then just moving onto the next person. You don't care about anyone."

Her voice had gotten louder and louder until she realized she'd been yelling.

Peter's face grew pale, as if she'd slapped him.

"Peter—I—"

"So that's what you think of me and my family? I didn't think you were like that. I thought we'd always been best friends."

They stood in front of Miss Evelyn's house. Peter glanced at Miss Evelyn, waiting on the front porch and avoided Caroline's eyes. "If that's what you really think, guess I'm glad I know that now." He turned on his heels and walked away fast.

Caroline's hands had left wet prints all over the spines of her books and small drops on the cover of the top one. She wiped them off on her dress as she made her way to the house.

Her face burned awfully bad.

Oh, why had she said so much?

"You're mighty quiet today."

Caroline looked up at the pair of socks she was darning. Or trying to darn. The material was coming apart more after she started, and the hole in the heel was growing wider. She sighed.

She never had been good with any kind of sewing or handiwork when it came to clothes.

Miss Evelyn chuckled. "Put that down. Don't worry about it. Not like I need to worry about socks yet anyhow, hot as it is."

Caroline threw the sock in the pile with the other clothes that needed mending. Thank goodness. That was one job she just couldn't do.

"That friend of yours, is he mistreating you?"

"Who? Peter? Oh, no, I just kinda got annoyed. That's all."

Miss Eveyln gave her a dark look. "Hope he's not involved."

"Involved with—?"

"With my husband."

"But—didn't you say he's dead?"

Miss Evelyn stopped rocking her chair. "That doesn't mean he didn't leave others to do his work. He had people looking for me. Searching for me and the kids."

"That was a long time ago, though. I'm sure no one is now. Who'd be paying them?"

"There are ways. I just hope you're not involved. You're not, are you?"

What was Miss Evelyn talking about? She was having one of her odd moments. The heat must've made her think strange things. Poor lady—what was it like to be that confused? To be so unsure that you couldn't trust anyone?

Caroline patted Miss Evelyn's hand. "Of course I'm not." She picked up one of her books from underneath her chair. "I brought something different to read today."

"'Now and then women should do for themselves what men have already done—occasionally what men have not done—thereby establishing themselves as person, and perhaps encouraging other women toward greater independence of thought and action. Some such consideration was a contributing reason for my wanting to do what I so much wanted to do.'"

Caroline paused from reading. Miss Evelyn, of course had already dozed off. Caroline smiled and shut the book. Amelia Earhart was so brave and stubborn. So much like Jo in *Little Women*. People like them knew what they wanted and went after it. No wonder Aunt June owned a copy of the book.

And George. George had always wanted to do something big, to leave Ripley and explore. Was Caroline like that, too? Was that why she loved characters like Jo?

Caroline leaned her head against the back of the chair. She'd never thought of it much before—she was only a child to Mama—but did she want to marry early like Blanche and the rest of the women in the family? Or would it be better to be adventurous, for a while anyway? To travel, or go to college, or try something completely different?

Her head ached with all the questions. Miss Evelyn snored. Caroline put her legs up in the chair and rocked back and forth. It didn't really matter what she wanted right now, though. Right now was what mattered right now. And right now meant she had to do what Mama couldn't do, and what Papa wasn't there to do.

She shut her eyes. It was only too bad she couldn't have more help doing it all.

He had been so quiet, standing in the shadows of the trees, that she would've walked by without ever spotting him if he hadn't spoken first.

"How's your sis doing, kiddo?"

Caroline almost dropped her books and looked around. Robert stepped out of the trees and out onto the road on her left side. "Oh, hello."

Robert grinned. His hair was all matted, his face unshaven. "You know, it's a real shame we won't get to be family now. You an I, we're kinda alike."

She shifted her weight and looked down at the road. What did Robert want? Why was he acting happy and smiling? "I'm—I'm sorry, Robert. I—I—don't really know what to say."

"Neither did Blanche." Robert spat on the ground. "She didn't know what to say either when I learned she'd been running around like some wild slut all summer. In the fields. In the backs of cars. My friend's car. He didn't know what to say either when I done figured it out. 'Cept that they was already married."

Caroline felt tears behind her eyes. Why did Robert have to point out Blanche's mistakes to her? It wasn't her fault things hadn't worked out.

"You an I, we're kinda alike," Robert repeated. "We both get treated like damned fools. Always doing things for everyone, and always getting walked all over. The people we love run off with other people." He stepped closer. His breath stunk. It was a sour smell, an alcohol smell. "Peter isn't interested in you. Thought he was the way he stared at you that night we danced. But he's just like your sister."

Now the tears almost spilled over. They were sad tears. Sad and frustrated ones. But Caroline told herself that they were hot, angry tears. It was easier to be angry.

"Maybe you should've talked to my sister about all of this. I'm sorry. I don't have anything I really need to say to you."

For a moment, it seemed as if he'd try to keep her there talking. Instead, he only put his hands in his pockets. Now he had tears dripping down his face.

"Tell your sister I still love her. I'll always love her. And the family." His voice was slurred.

"I'm so sorry for you. Good-bye," Caroline whispered. She walked away and didn't look back.

He would still be there, looking like a little child, overcome with loss, if she did.

Somehow, none of them heard the shot. Maybe it was too far away. But late in the night, no one, not even Mama, missed the loud banging on the door. Caroline stumbled in the darkness and scorched her finger on the match as she lit the candle in her room.

Mama came out into the hallway, feeling along the walls until she reached the staircase. Caroline held the candle closer so Mama could see it was her.

"What's going on?" Mama asked. Her eyes were so wide they seemed to take up her whole pale face.

"I don't know. I'll go find out. Why don't you check on Phoebe?" Caroline placed the candle in Mama's shaky hands and squinted in the dim light of Aunt Elsmere's lantern to get downstairs.

She and Aunt Elsmere reached the door at the same time. Before either one could open it, it opened from outside. Annie, Peter's sister who was a couple of years older than Phoebe, rushed in. Dirt and tears streaked her face.

"My heavens, what's wrong, child?" Aunt Elsmere put her arm around her. She handed Caroline the lantern. Annie looked from one of them to the other, panting. She must've run all the way there.

"Annie, what's wrong?" Caroline asked.

"It's Peter—" her voice shook. "He's been shot!"

Caroline almost dropped the lantern.

Aunt Elsmere acted as Caroline's mouth. She wiped Annie's face. "There, there. Breathe deeply. Where is he? Is he okay?"

Of course, he wasn't okay. She should've asked if he was still alive.

Annie's whole body shook. "He's over by the cat lady's house."

Caroline froze. "Miss Evelyn?"

Annie nodded, a fresh stream of tears running down her face. "Debra Jean stayed with him. Some of the other kids, they're scared, and they ran home. An older boy, I don't know his name, but he said you gotta put pressure on where he was hit. He took his shirt off and has it holding on him. They told me to run for help."

Aunt Elsmere looked as if she was about to vomit. "Do you know who shot him?"

Now Caroline's stomach turned. It was obvious who had shot him, wasn't it? Why else would Annie run all the way to their home when Miss Evelyn's was right there? What would happen to Miss Evelyn, who everyone always misunderstood? Had she been awakened during the night and mistaken Peter for a squirrel? Had she had another odd moment and thought it was a spy in her yard?

Annie shook her head. She wobbled. Aunt Elsmere held her by the shoulder. "Here, sit down." Annie sat at the bottom of the stairs.

Aunt Elsmere turned to Caroline. "I don't know what to do," she whispered. "We have no phone. Doctor Reynold lost his phone last week. He couldn't afford it anymore."

Caroline's heart thumped in her chest. What was Aunt Elsmere saying? Was there nothing they could do? It was clear that Aunt Elsmere was fighting not to lose control in front of Annie. Annie was too busy crying to notice even if she had.

"Dr. Reynold's home is nearly three miles away. We have no way to reach him," she muttered.

Caroline shook her head. There had to be a way. "I'll run the half mile to Peter's house. His dad can take a horse."

Aunt Elsmere nodded. But the doubt in her eyes spoke for itself. There wouldn't be enough time.

Was it already too late?

Caroline fell and scraped her hands. She jumped up and started running—almost tripping again. Even in the bright moonlight, it was hard to see where she was going.

Light came from the bend around the road. Car lights.

Caroline's heart raced. She ran to the road, screaming and waving her hands. "Stop! Please, please, stop!"

The car slammed its brakes on.

"Geez, kid, what do ya think you're doing?"

"Wait, it's Caroline!"

"Blanche! Thank God." Caroline shielded the light from her eyes and moved to the side of the car. "Blanche, it's Peter. He's been shot. I don't know how bad. He's between our house and Miss Evelyn's. Please. Go get him and take him to Doctor Reynold's."

Just then she noticed the man beside Blanche. Tall, muscular, dark hair. Kenneth.

"Hop in. We'll go right now." His voice was calm and steady now.

"Get in." Blanche grabbed her hand and helped her inside.

Then the car moved as if it was flying.

Splotches of blood stained the top of Peter's old white swimming shirt that was thrown aside on the ground. The boy who sat next to Peter used his own shirt to put pressure on the wound. It was also smeared with spots of red. He moved the shirt back some. Peter didn't seem to be bleeding anymore, but it was hard to tell where the bullet had hit, or how deep the injury was because of all the dried blood.

Peter's glazed eyes darted back and forth. His face shone a dull gray color.

Kenneth and one of the boys lifted Peter into the backseat. Blanche put her sweater under his head like a pillow.

"I want to come too," Caroline started getting in the car again.

"There's not enough room. I think you need to be with his sisters."

Caroline looked in Blanche's eyes. She was right. Peter's parents still didn't know. She nodded. A moment later, Kenneth's car was already out of sight.

"Come on. Let's go back to my house. We'll see Annie." Caroline tried to keep her voice even, the way Aunt Elsmere had, the way Kenneth had. "It will be okay," she whispered.

Caroline held onto Debra Jean's hand, just as she would've with Phoebe. The air felt hot, even in the darkness, and she felt even hotter from running. But Peter had been right about one thing—in the full moon, you could see pretty good. Good enough to play baseball. Good enough to aim at something, or someone, and shoot.

Goosebumps suddenly formed on her arms.

Was it Miss Evelyn who had shot? It *had* to be. Who else was around? Well, no one had thought that through, not Aunt Elsmere, not Blanche and Kenneth—no one had wondered what would happen if the person who shot was still nearby.

There were several boys walking home right now, and they had a farther way to go than she did. What if one of them got shot, and there was no one to run for help?

Caroline paused. The only sounds were the crickets and Debra Jean's whimpering.

"Debra Jean," Caroline bent down so she was eye level with her. "Did you see who did this to Peter? Do you know what happened?"

Debra Jean shrugged. "I was playing marbles with Annie. We wasn't really watching the boys. All of a sudden we heard a shot." She started shaking. "We heard another shot, then a scream. We ran to see what happened. Peter was bloody and yelling. Then he knocked out."

Caroline's breath caught in her throat. Two shots. It couldn't have been some kind of accident then. Miss Evelyn's aim was usually right on, but she was old. It was dark.

Debra Jean squeezed Caroline's hand. "You don't think he's dead, do you?"

Caroline sighed and brushed back a piece of Debra Jean's dirty hair from her face. It was like the time Phoebe asked about George. How could you give an answer to something no one could know?

"I hope not, Debra Jean. I hope not."

At least one thing was for sure. Miss Evelyn wouldn't leave her own property. She wouldn't be coming after anyone.

But when her crazy spell went away, what would she say when she found out what she'd done?

When they got home, Aunt Elsmere was in the kitchen warming some of Phoebe's soup for Annie. "Here, come get something nice to eat," she said to Debra Jean. She gave her a place to sit, then pulled Caroline aside.

She wore an odd look on her face as Caroline told her about running into Blanche. That look of trying not to sneeze.

"Well, do you think he'll live?"

Again, one of those questions.

Caroline didn't try to answer. Her eyes finally gave into crying, and she left the room before the girls could see.

Then she cried into her pillow for as long as she could.

What would happen to Peter? If he lived, it didn't matter if he never held her hand again, or if he never even spoke to her again. She deserved it for taking her anger out on him. It only mattered that he *did* live. He was her best friend, just as he'd said. And maybe she'd ruined that by trying to be older. By trying to be something they weren't ready for, or maybe something they weren't meant to be.

Her head ached, and her eyes burned. She couldn't lose Peter.

She had been his Jo.

And he had been her Laurie.

Chapter 15

Whispers came from downstairs. Or maybe it just sounded far away. It was hard to tell.

Something clung to the inside of Caroline's mouth, on her tongue and sides of her mouth. Hair. And no wonder— somehow her face had smashed into the pillow. Why was she lying there like that? She moved. Her neck ached. Her head felt dizzy. Had she been in one single position the whole night?

Then it all flooded back to her: the pounding on the door; Annie crying; Peter getting shot; running through the darkness; meeting Kenneth; the car ride; the awful walk home; and trying to hold herself together.

She rolled over on her back. What time was it? She had overslept. The sun was bright. She couldn't remember even falling asleep. Or when the crying ended so she could fall asleep.

Caroline stood up. Her elbow bumped into the oak chifferobe, sending a tingling pain through her arm. She rubbed it and glanced in the mirror above the chest of drawers. Her face looked puffy from crying so long and so hard. Some drops of blood had splattered onto the bottom of her nightgown. Peter's blood.

Somehow, she looked older. How could a person look older over one night? It didn't make sense, but, somehow, she did. Somehow, she looked different from the girl who'd been angry at Peter the day before.

She tied her hair with a ribbon and didn't bother brushing out the tangles. She threw on a dress and went to the door.

Her hand froze on the knob. Did she really want to go downstairs and find out what had happened? What if it was the news she was dreading? What if Peter had died during the night?

What about Miss Evelyn? How could she do such a thing? Was she going to have to spend the rest of her old, lonely life in jail?

Maybe Caroline could lock the door and bury her face in the pillow once more. Maybe she could just stay there and not ever leave. She could shut all the bad things out and not answer anyone. Nothing could reach her and hurt her if she stayed away.

But that would be exactly what Mama had done, wouldn't it? She had tried to lock all the horrible things out of her life. And she'd locked the good things out, too.

She stood there a long time.

No, she didn't want this dazed, sad feeling to stay. She didn't want to miss seeing Phoebe get better, or miss hugging Papa when he came home. In the end, maybe it would be better knowing what had happened. She took a deep breath.

When she got downstairs, the sitting room was full. Aunt Elsmere and Blanche and Kenneth and Aunt June and Uncle P. Joe and Thomas and Pamelia and even Mama—they were all there staring at her when she came down.

Her vision shook for a second. Blanche looked as if she'd been crying or throwing up. Or both.

"Come here, sweetie," Aunt June got up from her place at Mama's secretary and came toward her with a glass of tea. "The ice man came early today. Isn't that a treat?" She opened the tin ice bucket and scooped out a couple of tiny pieces of ice, more wet than solid.

Caroline's tongue was very dry, she realized. She gulped the tea down. It was cool and gentle on her parched throat.

"What happened?"

Aunt June glanced around the room. Uncle P. Joe got up from his chair so she could have a place to sit, but Caroline shook her head and whispered, "No, thanks. What happened to Peter?"

"Don't worry. Peter's still alive," Aunt June said, patting her arm. "He got stitched up right away. The bullet missed his chest and hit his arm instead, more like glazed it. That's what Dr. Reynold said when he came by to see Phoebe."

So Peter was alive. Caroline sat down Indian-style on the cool floor and continued drinking the tea. Relief washed over her. Her whole body seemed to let go—of what, she didn't know. It was as if she'd been holding on to something. Now, she felt achy.

A good ache. Peter was alive.

The only sound in the room for the next few minutes were Caroline's loud swallows. With every sip she took, it felt as if she was slowly coming back to normal. Every sip reassured Peter was alive—how could he not be?

Caroline set her empty glass on the wooden floor with a clunk. Aunt June refilled it.

Kenneth's eyes met hers. They were soft blue, like her own, "the Neal eyes," as Papa always pointed out. His hair was dark like Thomas's, his arms big and strong, not thin the way George's had always been. He glanced down at the floor. It must have been awkward to sit there, knowing everyone in the room didn't really want him.

Mama was studying him, her face blank. What did she think of him, this new member of the family? What did they all think of him?

They sat there so quiet. Pamelia rubbed her growing belly. Mama stared at everyone. Blanche kept twisting her fingers and not looking anyone in the eye. Every other minute, she'd wipe her face with her fingers, trying not to cry. Then she'd go back to twisting them.

It was impossible to tell what they thought of Kenneth. But he'd helped save Peter's life.

For Caroline that was enough to give him a chance. He wasn't Robert, but he was there in their lives, whether they liked it or not.

Aunt June poured Caroline another glass of tea and handed her a big fluffy buttered biscuit with it. "Eat something bland. It'll make you feel better. You look as weak as water."

Aunt Elsmere rocked back and forth in the rocker at the corner of the room. She looked more tired than ever before. Her hair had more gray than black. "June, that makes no sense—water ain't that weak. Least it wasn't when it took my house down."

The rocking chair creaked against the wooden floor, the way the clock on the mantelpiece used to tick so evenly before the battery broke, but it stopped. Everyone looked at Mama. Had she picked up on that comment about the floods? Was she going to start crying about George?

"The girls ended up staying the night," Aunt Elsmere continued, rocking once more, before Mama had time to react. "They went home early this morning. Poor things."

Caroline took a bite of the biscuit. Aunt June passed her some strawberry jam to spread on it. Her mouth was still dry, and there was a chalky feeling after she swallowed, as it did when bits of dirt flew in her mouth and nostrils when she worked in the fields during a draught.

Half of the room was in the shadows already, and the big oak tree, the one she read under, cast its silhouette across the floor. Its leaves sprinkled another layer of pattern over the red, brown, and orange checkered sofa and Mama's intricate floral cross-stitch above the fireplace.

"What time is it?"

"It's past noon," Pamelia said softly.

"It's almost four o'clock," Thomas said.

Then Caroline noticed everyone else's empty plates. Chicken bones on one, some bits of cornbread on another.

They'd finished dinner already. Probably a couple of hours before.

Even Mama's plate was pretty empty. At least she'd eaten something.

"It's okay. You needed your rest," Aunt Elsmere said. "After all, Peter's your best friend.

"I know it was hard on all of us, but especially you. You were very brave. You calmed Debra Jean down so much, it was easy getting her to go sleep."

It was rare to hear such a thing from Aunt Elsmere. Caroline took another biscuit and began spreading more jam on it, several spoonfuls so it wouldn't be as dry. She felt hungry. And awake now. It was good to be in the room with all of them.

Mama's eyes met hers for just a moment. Then she went back to staring at Kenneth.

But Kenneth was sitting there, like one of the family already, even if he wasn't welcomed by everyone. It couldn't have been the way Blanche wanted it, but at least they'd all met him now.

Blanche's face looked slightly green. Why did she act so miserable?

"Blanche?" Caroline put down her biscuit. "What—what's wrong?"

They all avoided looking at her now. Kenneth put his arm around Blanche.

It was Aunt Elsmere who spoke. "Why don't *you* tell her, Blanche? Or you, Kenneth? Why don't you go on and tell her what happened?"

Blanche started bawling. "It's my fault. It's all my fault." She stood up and left the room.

Kenneth rolled his eyes. "Was that necessary? Are you really going to hold this over her? Torment her for her whole life?"

He glared at Aunt Elsmere and left the room. The front door slammed behind him.

Now Aunt Elsmere twisted her hands in her lap. "Well, I don't know what the rest of you think. But I don't stand for this mess. Not one bit. That poor boy—I never. I just can't take it."

She went upstairs.

Caroline's throat closed up. They said Peter was fine, so what was wrong?

Aunt June put her hand on Caroline's shoulder. "Honey, Miss Evelyn—"

"Oh, no!" Caroline cried. She'd forgotten Miss Evelyn, sitting there feeling relieved. How could she be eating when Miss Evelyn had done something so awful? "I—I knew she shoots squirrels and talks about spies and her dead husband. I guess I should've done something. I just thought she was old. She *is* old, but she's not as bad as I thought—"

"It's not what you think," Aunt June said. "Miss Evelyn—well—she didn't cause the accident, like, like some of us wondered at first."

Caroline felt relief spread through her again. Her legs felt tingly as the sudden tension left. "She didn't? But—what happened then?"

Aunt June cleared her throat, glancing in Mama's direction. "Miss Evelyn came outside this morning and called the police when she realized what went on."

Miss Evelyn must've been scared out of her wits if she used her phone.

"She—she found Robert—oh, there's no easy way to say it. She found Robert near her tomato garden. Dead." Her voice trailed off at the end. But that last word clung in the silent room.

Dead? The word stayed that way for just a moment—dead. Caroline had only seen Robert the day before. He wasn't dead. How could he be dead? Why in Miss Eveyln's yard?

"Y'all are wrong. I saw Robert, and he wasn't dead. He was mad, but he wasn't dead."

Caroline clenched her fists and didn't notice that she'd knocked her glass over until she sat in a puddle, the tops of her legs and panties soaked.

They all stared at her. No one said anything.

"Well, don't look at me like that. That's the most blasted idea. Robert's not dead. He's not."

Thomas cleared his throat. "Don't shout. It's confusing to us too. All we know is what the police said earlier. They found Robert near Miss Evelyn's tomatoes."

Caroline wanted to laugh all of a sudden. "Just sitting there, dead?" Then she remembered the fear from the night before. Maybe whoever shot Peter had shot Robert too. "But why was Robert even at Miss Evelyn's? He wasn't playing ball. And why would someone shoot him *and* Peter? And get away with it? Why would anyone do something like this?"

Thomas stared at the floor. "All we know is that he had a gun in his hand—and a bullet in his head."

Tears filled Caroline's eyes. She stifled a scream with her hand. "Gun? You mean—you mean—you think he shot himself? He killed himself? Robert *shot* himself?"

Mama got down on the floor beside Caroline and held her. They both cried, Mama rocking her back and forth. Pamelia went across the room and held Mama's hand. It was as if Mama had lost another son. It was as if Caroline had lost another brother.

For the longest time, no one said anything. The only sounds in that room were sad ones, ones of grief, ones of regret, and ones that couldn't understand something so terrible.

Well, Debra Jean said it had been *two* shots.

"*In the fields. In the backs of cars. My friend's car.*" That's what Robert had said. Barely twenty-four hours ago. Had Robert been drunk and waiting in Miss Evelyn's field? Had he been so angry he wanted to shoot Kenneth but instead shot Peter when he was searching for his baseball?

Robert's sad face wouldn't leave Caroline. She probably knew more than the rest of them, yet she'd never know anything really. It would *never* make sense. It couldn't possibly *ever* make sense that someone could do such a thing.

What would George say when he got home and found out his closest friend was dead? But was George dead too? Was he never going to come home?

It was too much.

Mama held her the way she sometimes held Phoebe. Caroline buried her face in Mama's shoulder. She wanted to sit there, wrapped in Mama's arms, like a baby, forever.

Twenty-two years old and dead. Robert had lost the lady he'd loved for years, and he must've thought he'd killed an innocent boy.

No wonder he'd decided to give up, to close the door forever.

Yet she'd *never* understand why he had.

Aunt June knocked on the bedroom door again.

"Are you okay? Don't you want some supper?"

Caroline groaned into her pillow.

"Caroline?"

"I'm fine. I'm not hungry. I'm going to bed early."

It was silent in the hallway.

"Okay. I'll be going on home, I guess. I'll see you tomorrow."

A minute later, Aunt June was walking down the stairs. Caroline rolled over on her side and stared out the window. The sun was just starting to grow dark.

Tomorrow. That was a word everyone seemed to take for granted. A word *she* hadn't really thought about till now. It was a word that assumed an awful lot. A word that made promises no one could keep.

Who knew what would happen tomorrow? Or the many tomorrows after that? Yesterday at this time, Peter hadn't been hurt. Robert hadn't been dead.

Caroline pulled the sheet over her body, then over her head. She couldn't block out Robert's pathetic, drunken face. Maybe it would always be in her mind, haunting her everywhere she went. It was just as much her fault as it was Blanche's that he was dead, after all. Wasn't it?

Maybe if she had told someone Robert was drinking. Maybe if she'd stayed and talked to him, or invited him inside until he sobered up. Maybe if she'd mentioned Blanche's running off. Maybe if she'd just talked to Blanche instead of getting mad and arguing with her.

She curled into a tight ball.

Maybe.

She'd never know for sure, though. Maybe there was nothing anyone could have done to stop him. The worse part about it was that they'd never know.

A wasp hit the outside screen. Even under the sheets, Caroline could tell it was a wasp without looking up. She'd heard enough wasps hit their wings against that screen before. They liked to build nests right above it.

Suddenly, she stifled a laugh in the sheets.

How funny was it that things went on like normal? That wasps still built nests? That Ripley still went about its business? Hot and tired, like one giant set of blistered hands picking cotton.

It just kept going, no matter who left, or who died.

Just a few hours ago, Caroline had tried to prepare herself in case Peter had been killed.

Instead, it was Robert, and she wasn't prepared at all. *Would* she have been ready if it was Peter, though? Or Phoebe? Or George?

How did anyone prepare?

How did anyone ever go back to normal when something like this happened? Caroline rocked her curled up body back and forth. For the first time that summer, she wasn't hot. She wasn't cold either.

She just was.

Chapter 16

It was nearly half past ten when Caroline woke again the next morning. She lay in bed, and one after another, all the bad thoughts from the day before flooded through her.

She wiped her eyes.

This wouldn't do.

She couldn't stay in bed forever and feel bad about something she couldn't change. There was plenty of work, and Aunt Elsmere wouldn't be able to do it alone.

Caroline dressed and splashed some water on her face.

When she got downstairs, Blanche was in the kitchen making a later breakfast, or early dinner. Something smelled as if it was burning. Blanche fumbled with a skillet when Caroline entered the room.

"Morning. Thought I'd help fix some food," Blanche mumbled.

About time you did something, Caroline wanted to say.

Instead she nodded. "Where'd you stay last night?"

Blanche's face turned red. "Oh, I—well, I stayed with Kenneth. We've been staying in Elsa Mae's guest room, just until we leave."

Caroline nodded.

"Just thought it was better that way. With everything—everything that's gone on."

Again, Caroline nodded. It *was* better that way.

Blanche took some cornbread out of the oven. Sure enough, its edges looked a little black. She sighed and held the skillet in one hand and rubbed her eyes with the other. She had dark circles underneath. She seemed dull and paler than normal. Even her hair seemed flat and not perky the way it usually was.

Caroline needed to stay there, to help Blanche in case she started feeling sick. To help Aunt Elsmere with Phoebe. To help Uncle P. Joe and Thomas chop cotton.

But she didn't want to. She couldn't.

"I'm going to visit Miss Evelyn."

Blanche had turned the skillet over, but the bread stuck to it and wouldn't come out. She looked up at Caroline, her eyes wide.

But she didn't say anything. She nodded.

The bread fell from the skillet, one big, crumbled mess.

"Do you want something to eat first?"

Caroline shook her head. "No, thanks."

Caroline didn't know which way to take when she stepped out on the front porch. She put her hands over her eyes and let them adjust to the sunlight.

If she took the road, she'd cross the spot where she'd last seen Robert. If she cut through the fields, it would remind her of the accident.

In the end, she took the road. If she was going to remember Robert, and, obviously, she always would, it was best to think of him alive, not dead. When she arrived at the spot where he'd been, she ran until she got in front of Miss Evelyn's house.

Miss Evelyn sat on her rocker.

"Well, I'd been wondering when you'd come by. Worried you'd forgotten about an ugly old lady like me." She shoved a big bowl of peanuts in Caroline's arms.

"I knew you'd come by. Somehow, I just knew you would. Far too hot to do anything real busy today. My daughter sent me several huge sacks of these nuts." She grunted. "Guess she thinks if I've got some nuts, it erases the fact I haven't seen her in ten years. Maybe she's trying to tell me she thinks *I'm* nuts." She grunted again. "She ain't the only one. Anyhow, we'll shell 'em and make peanut butter out of them. You can take as many of them home as you please."

Caroline smiled for the first time in a couple of days, and it felt wonderful. Who would have thought Miss Evelyn would be the one to make her feel better?

But she did. She did because she seemed to know Caroline didn't want to talk about any of the bad things that had happened. That she didn't need to talk about them quite yet.

Maybe Miss Evelyn didn't want to talk about them either.

So they didn't.

They sat there, a couple of hours, not saying much, just shelling peanuts. Miss Evelyn said to eat as many as she wanted, so Caroline ate several handfuls. She hadn't eaten since the biscuit the afternoon before, and the peanuts tasted good and crunchy, and, somehow, she felt stronger after she ate a bunch.

"You're dripping wet," Miss Evelyn said after a while. "My goodness, it's hot." She fanned her face with the fan she always kept outside. "If you step inside, there's a pitcher of lemonade in the kitchen."

Caroline hadn't paid much attention to the heat, even though Miss Evelyn later said her thermostat showed it was the hottest day they'd had that whole year—one hundred and three degrees.

Her dress was so wet from just sitting there that she could have rung it out. Her head ached before she drank almost the whole pitcher of lemonade. But Caroline went through the afternoon in a daze.

They didn't do much of anything, just sat and shelled those nuts. They didn't read. They didn't make peanut butter. Miss Evelyn said it was just too hot.

Did she even know how to make peanut butter?

Probably not.

They didn't even bother sweeping up their mess of peanut shells. Before she left, Miss Evelyn finally asked about Peter. "How's your friend?"

"He's okay. I mean, that's what I was told."

Miss Evelyn raised her white, bushy eyebrows. "You haven't gone to visit him?"

"Well, the last time I saw him, we argued."

"Oh, but there's still time. Don't let that be the last time."

Caroline started to ask what that meant, but Miss Evelyn pursed her lips together, knowingly. Then she ate another handful of nuts.

Caroline stopped at the pond, *their* swimming place, and waded into the water. It was so hot, the water wasn't even that refreshing. Not cool as normal. She went in until the water reached her chest. Then she glanced around and ducked her head underneath.

It felt good getting her hair soaked. She stayed under as long as she could, until she needed air. She came up and floated on her back, staring up into the sky.

The sunlight poured through the thick tree branches and danced on top of the canopy of bright green leaves. The water in her ears made any noise around her foggy. Her limbs hung limply, floating.

If she could sleep like this, in a bed of water, she'd probably sleep very well.

Caroline stood up so that she *wouldn't* fall asleep. She swam back to the shallow end and sat on the bottom, with only her head poking out from the water.

She remembered the way Aunt Elsmere had fussed the last time she'd been swimming, the *only* time that summer she'd been swimming.

Caroline looked down. Her chest just barely poked out. Just enough to where she could see the outline of her breasts, two small, soft points. She put her hands over them and cupped them in her fingers, covering them up, as if someone was there—as if Peter was there with her.

She made sure the mud was rinsed off the bottom of her dress before she got out of the water. Then she squeezed her dripping hair and sat in the sunshine with her eyes closed, letting it soak inside her.

She breathed deeply. No sound. Just the water. It had been a good idea to leave the house for a while. To get away.

Only now, Caroline missed Peter more than she ever had.

She would've turned around and gone back home, if both Annie and Debra Jean hadn't been sitting on the porch playing a game of marbles.

Debra Jean pulled her thumb out of her mouth and ran down the steps to meet her as she got closer. She wrapped her arms around Caroline in a big hug.

When they reached the porch, Annie stood up and gave her a hug, too.

"Peter's in his room, but I can go see if he's awake," Annie said.

Caroline pulled on the neckline of her dress—damp, but already almost dry—away from her body, airing it out more.

"Oh, well, that's okay. If he's resting, I'll come back another time."

Annie and Debra Jean looked at each other.

"Well, he really wants to see you," Debra Jean said. "He misses you."

"He—he does?"

"Well, that's what he said. He slept a lot yesterday, and he's been resting. He's real sore. Doctor said that shot knocked him down. Made him really scared too, so he has to have lots of rest," Annie started placing the marbles into a little, drawstring sack.

"He said we could wake him up if you came by. He was worried you might not ever come." Debra Jean held onto Caroline's hand, as if she were her new hero after their walk back home that night.

Caroline felt the redness seep all over, not just her face, but her whole body. She felt even hotter now, hotter than she had during the brightest point of the day when she'd been with Miss Evelyn.

Her hair was still damp and matted against her head and neck. She hadn't eaten much in the last couple of days, so she probably looked even thinner than normal. And the last time she'd seen Peter, she'd yelled at him.

Yet, he wanted to see her.

Caroline swallowed hard. "Okay, well, if your mother's okay with it, can I go inside and see him?"

Annie opened the front door. "Mama was feeding the baby, but she said she was going to take a nap afterwards."

Debra Jean pulled her hand, "Come on inside."

When they entered the living room, Debra Jean backed away.

"Aren't y'all coming too?"

They both shook their heads.

"He said not to," Annie said, the corners of her lips turning up.

"Oh, okay. Well, I'll just be a few minutes then." Caroline walked up the stairs, tiptoeing past the room she knew belonged to their parents, as if she did this all the time. As if she came to Peter's room whenever she wanted to. When she was younger, they'd played in each other's bedrooms from time to time, but she hadn't set foot in the upstairs of his house for at least two years.

Her heart pounded. Her hand froze on the door knob. Should she knock? What if he was asleep?

Why did she have to be so nervous? It was only Peter.

But so much had changed, even in the last two days.

Caroline breathed deeply and fanned her face. She gently pushed the door open. Peter lay there with his head tilted to one side, eyes closed, mouth slightly open. Beneath his shirt, there was a large, white bandage poking out, just above his collar bone.

She would have turned around and walked away right then, but, somehow she couldn't. It was too much to see him lying there, when he, too, could have been killed. If the bullet had struck maybe just two or three inches over, he would have been.

A chair had been moved beside the bed. Was it there for her? No, it must've been because they'd all been talking to him and checking on him.

Caroline walked over and sat down anyhow. She felt like crying, but, somehow, the tears weren't there. Peter's big, calloused hands rested at his sides, open, fingers slightly apart. Caroline stared at those hands a long time. When she finally tore her eyes away from them and looked at Peter's face, he was watching her.

His eyes were the ones that looked watery.

"I was so worried I wouldn't see you again," he said softly, almost whispering.

"Peter." Without thinking, Caroline reached over and hugged him. "Oh, sorry, did I hurt you? I'm sorry."

"No, no, you're okay." Peter fanned his face. "Lord, it's hot."

"A hundred and three degrees. That's what Miss Evelyn said earlier." Caroline looked down in her lap. That's where she'd been going the day they'd argued too.

Peter didn't mention it. "Gosh, that's hot." Then he slipped her hand into his.

Caroline's face had to be bright pink—how could it not be? But Peter's wasn't. He sat there talking, as if he hadn't done anything different at all. How was it that he was so calm and made things look easy? She couldn't even hug him without being awkward about it.

She interrupted whatever he was saying. "Peter—look—I know you won't say anything about it, but I'm sorry. I'm sorry for the way I got mad and yelled the other day."

Peter rubbed the palm of her hand with his thumb in a circular motion. "I'm not mad at you. I was more mad at myself."

"Why?"

"Well, you were right. I was kind of a jerk. And I'm sorry I gave you the wrong idea. Look, Anna and I are friends, but—I promise that's nothing—nothing else."

Caroline sighed and glanced around the room. It wasn't as messy as it used to be. Peter still had all of his model boats and airplanes sitting on top of his chifferobe and the desk in the corner.

"Caroline—I—you'll always be really important to me. When I woke up in the backseat of that car, with my head in Blanche's lap, I was in so much pain. But I didn't wonder why I was there, or understand what had happened. I only thought I was going to die."

Caroline's eyes filled up with tears, but they didn't spill over.

"I cried myself to sleep," she whispered. "Because I thought you were, too."

Peter pulled the neckline of his shirt down. The bandage covered his whole shoulder area. "There's a big gash on my shoulder, but I didn't know it wasn't as serious as it could've been."

Caroline nodded.

Peter put her fingers between his. "I was worried I'd never

see you again. Then all day yesterday I hoped you come by. When you didn't—I worried you were still mad at me."

"I—I wanted to, but, well, I—I guess you heard about Robert."

Peter's face clouded over. "Yeah, I did. I'm so—"

"Shocked."

"Yes. I'm sorry. I know he was good friends with George."

"He was."

They sat there in silence for a while, hand-in-hand. Caroline would've stayed longer, but Debra Jean came upstairs to see whether Peter wanted ham or chicken for supper.

"I need to get home," Caroline said, pulling her hand away.

"Oh, okay." Peter sat up. "I'll walk you out. I wanted to give you something."

When they stepped outside, Peter led her to the barn. He went inside and came back with the grey kitten in the arm opposite the side with the bandage. It looked a pound or so bigger, but it was still tiny. It licked Peter's hand with its pink tongue.

"I wanted you to have your kitten," he said. "I think it's ready for its new home now."

Caroline held it the way Peter's mother held the baby, cradled in her arm. It licked her, and its whiskers tickled.

"Thank you."

"You're welcome." Peter had his hands in his pockets. He looked as if he wanted to say something, but he didn't.

"I'll see you later."

She walked to the road.

"Caroline!"

She turned around. Peter still stood there, hands in his pockets.

"I'm glad you came," he said.

"I am too."

She smiled the whole way home.

Chapter 17

Mama had eaten almost a whole baked potato by herself. She poked around her plate, scraping the potato skin clean.

It was a small thing. Such a small thing it was silly to feel as glad about it as Caroline did. But Mama hadn't been eating or talking or doing normal in so long.

Caroline wasn't the only one watching her. They sat there, eating quietly, afraid of breaking the spell and causing Mama to get upset and want to go home.

Aunt June opened up her china cabinet and pulled down one of her fine crystal bowls.

"Auntie, you really don't have to go to any trouble," Blanche said.

Aunt June gave her a firm look. Her lips were pressed together, and her eyebrows were raised.

Blanche smiled and shook her head. Her auburn curls looked shiny underneath the overhead light. Everything looked shiny when you had electric. Even the faded yellow daisy wallpaper was brighter than it was during the day.

They all sat there—Aunt June and Uncle P. Jo, Thomas and Pamelia, Blanche and Kenneth, and Caroline. Mama had finally left the house for the first time since she found out Pamelia was expecting.

Everyone was there except Phoebe and Aunt Elsmere.

The whole thing was Aunt June's idea. Even if Blanche hadn't had a wedding, she said, she deserved a family dinner to celebrate.

Aunt Elsmere insisted on staying with Phoebe. Really, she didn't want to be there. She'd never approve of any of it, no matter how many lives Kenneth helped save. Not even for

Blanche's sake. Blanche, who had always been Aunt Elsmere's favorite.

It was odd how one mistake had changed everything.

"Caroline, can you come help me and P. Joe a minute?"

Caroline coughed. She'd had a mouthful of carrots sitting in her mouth. Just sitting there because she'd forgotten to chew, she'd been so focused on everyone else.

She swallowed and took a sip of sweet tea. "Sure, of course."

She followed Aunt June into the kitchen.

The sunset streamed in through the one tiny window above the sink. The peach wallpaper looked gold in the light.

Aunt June lit a lantern. "I don't want to turn on the lights in here and have anyone coming in. Thought you'd be my best pick to help with a surprise." She moved the lantern over on the counter, next to the rack full of spices.

Caroline gasped. A three layered frosted cake with violet ribbon and bits of lavender and red roses on top sat on a silver platter with gold edges that she'd never seen in Aunt June's china cabinet before.

"Pulled it from the chest in my room. It's the platter my own cake was on. Thought I'd pass it on to Blanche so she'd have at least one fancy gift."

"Oh, Aunt June. She'll be so surprised." A wedding cake was probably the last thing on Blanche's mind now. The time and the cost were ridiculous with everything else going on.

"Of course, I couldn't forget," Aunt June said. Her red hair looked orange with the light from the walls reflecting off on it. "Took me all day to make, but I did it. Now, here, can you turn the ice cream while I go back in there before they notice?"

Aunt June set Caroline down on a wooden stool in the corner of the kitchen behind the table, where no one could really notice her if they came in. She took out her tin measuring cup and poured a couple of cups of milk, a cup of sorghum, some eggs, and a few other things into the inner bowl of the wooden ice cream maker and put the precious ice and salt in the outer bowl. She started turning the dasher around and around.

"Here, you take over." Aunt June placed Caroline's hand where hers had been. Then, she went back to the dining room.

Caroline turned the small handle until her hand was sore. Then she rotated hands. The whole time, she kept glancing over at the wedding cake.

It was good that at least one of Blanche's wedding dreams got to happen. It was good someone had remembered.

Of course, Aunt June wouldn't forget.

"Oh, Auntie. It's—oh, it's just perfect!"

Blanche wrapped her arms around Aunt June, hugging her so tight it seemed as if it would hurt.

Kenneth held up his glass, even though there wasn't anything inside it except ice water. He stood up. "I'd like to thank everyone for what you've done tonight. For celebrating with us and for making me feel welcome. It means an awful lot."

It was a short speech. Not really a speech. Caroline hadn't been to many weddings, but she knew that was too short.

Of course, he must've also known that part of the family hated him. How could he possibly feel welcomed?

Thomas never looked directly at Kenneth. Or Blanche. Pamelia didn't say much.

At least they were there, though. It was just going to take some getting used to, Caroline thought, while Aunt June took a photo of Blanche and Kenneth cutting the cake with the big, bulky camera she never used, except on special occasions.

Maybe it would be the way it was every time Caroline read *Little Women*. It was always disappointing when Jo turned down

Laurie and later ended up marrying Dr. Baer. He just never seemed quite as good as Laurie.

But by the time she finished the book and read *Little Men*, there didn't seem to be a better match.

Maybe Kenneth was like Dr. Baer.

Maybe they'd all just have to get used to him. And get to know him first.

Blanche wore a lovely navy dress that fell just below her knees. Her curls were swept back in a bun at the nape of her neck, and a little navy hat perched on top of her head. She wore blush on her cheeks and red lipstick on her lips.

Caroline sat on the bed with the new kitten between her and Phoebe, just as entranced as she was. Blanche was prettier even than she'd been at the Bisbee Show.

Phoebe tried sitting up, but coughed. It sounded deep and thick and painful. She rested her head back on the pillow. "When did you get a new dress?"

Blanche gazed into the mirror and puckered her lips. She applied one more coat of lipstick. "Kenneth gave it to me as one of my wedding gifts. He said every girl deserves a dress when she gets married."

Phoebe sighed. "I really wanted to be at your wedding. I thought we were gonna have a big party with cake and dancing." Her eyes were dark underneath. Her skin had gotten so pale, it appeared yellowish in the morning light. She looked like one of Miss Evelyn's small cats when it begged for milk to drink.

"I have some cake saved for you in the kitchen. When you feel better, you can eat it." Blanche's eyes met Caroline's. Blanche never knew how to talk to Phoebe the way she did.

But Caroline didn't say anything for her. How could she explain why there had been a wedding cake without a wedding?

"I'll never get to go dancing now," Phoebe wailed. "I'm gonna be trapped in this boy room my whole life!"

Blanche smiled and held Phoebe's hand. "That's not true. You're getting better a little every day. And this room is just like ours."

Which was true. The one real difference between Thomas and George's old room and the one they shared was that this one had red plaid curtains, instead of pink ones. It had two small beds, instead of one big one, and the mirror was smaller. Other than that, they were exactly the same, on the opposite ends of the house.

"You know what?" Blanche tucked a strand of hair behind Phoebe's ear. "Maybe now Mama and Papa will let you both have your own rooms. Maybe when I come back in the spring, I'll bring you some nice new curtains."

Phoebe nodded. Then she started coughing again.

Caroline swallowed hard. Why did Blanche have to say that? Why'd she have to try changing even more than she'd already changed? What if she didn't care about having the large bed to herself? What if she liked things the way they'd been? And why promise Phoebe something when it probably wouldn't happen?

After all, when George returned, he'd need his room back.

Kenneth drove up to the house and stopped in front of the porch. In the light, his car looked much shinier and newer than most cars Caroline had ridden in. It was far cleaner than Charles Jackson's old Model T. He wore a gray suit and tie that matched his eyes. His face was clean shaven.

Blanche wrapped her arm around his. The new dress twirled against her thin legs, and the waist made her look like an hour glass.

"I'm gonna run in real quick and say goodbye to Mama," Blanche said. She let go of Kenneth's arm.

Caroline sat down on the step. It didn't seem as if Blanche could be leaving. Would she really have a round belly soon like Peter's mother had?

It seemed impossible that Blanche could ever grow to be that size. It seemed more impossible that she'd have a baby and a family of her own, and Caroline wouldn't be there to be a part of it. She wouldn't be there to stoop down and pick things up once Blanche grew so large and couldn't reach them. She wouldn't be there to hold her hand when the baby was born.

Something patted Caroline on the back. She looked up from staring at the gray, wooden step and up into Kenneth's blue eyes.

"She's not gone for good," he said. "She'll just be gone while she's—expecting."

"You mean pregnant."

Kenneth bit his lip at the word.

He nodded. Beads of sweat formed on his forehead. It was a wonder he didn't pass out from wearing his suit. "I know this isn't what everyone planned on. I didn't plan on it either.

He sighed. "When I—when I first saw your sister, she was walking off this here porch. She was the prettiest thing I'd ever seen. I knew she had a date, and I had a date. But I thought, 'I'm gonna marry that girl,' anyway." He shrugged, maybe embarrassed he'd said too much. "I just knew it."

Caroline smiled. It was only too bad they couldn't have been honest when they started seeing each other. It was too bad they couldn't have waited on a lot of things.

He handed her a slip of paper. "Here's my folks' address. Write whenever you want. And we'll come visit once in a while. Or you can come see us."

Caroline nodded. Until the baby was born, she'd have to be the one to visit them, of course. That was the whole point in their going to Arkansas, so no one would suspect Blanche got pregnant before she was married.

Blanche came out on the porch. Her blush was streaked with tears.

"I'll be in the car," Kenneth said. He nodded goodbye to Caroline and walked away so they could have a moment.

If saying goodbye to Phoebe was hard, telling Mama goodbye must've been awful.

Caroline hugged Blanche and smoothed her hair with her hand.

"Oh, Caroline. I've made a huge mess of things."

"But you're married. And he really loves you."

Blanche hiccupped. "I know, and I love him too. But it shouldn't have happened this way."

Caroline held Blanche's shoulders. Part of her wanted to say that she was right. It shouldn't have happened this way. If Blanche had helped instead of running off all summer, maybe a lot of things would be different. If she'd been honest, maybe Robert wouldn't be dead.

But there was no use saying any of it.

"You know, I'm gonna miss you," she said instead.

Blanche's eyes filled again. "I'm gonna miss you too."

They stood there hugging each other, their hair in each other's' faces, their clothes getting damp with the heat of the sun rising higher, their hearts beating as fast as they could, beating together, so anxious they could almost be heard.

Finally, Blanche got in the car beside Kenneth. She waved goodbye until the car was a speck in the distance.

It was just like when Papa left.

Only now, Caroline sat on the porch alone.

Chapter 18

Mama cut a generous slice of watermelon.

"Here, Caroline." She set the watermelon on a plate and handed it to Caroline. In the light of the lantern, she smiled.

"Thank you." Caroline took the fruit and bit into it. Sweetness filled her mouth, thirsty from running and playing tag. Mama knew watermelon was her favorite part about the Fourth of July. Every year she let her choose which one they would serve.

Caroline spat out a mouthful of seeds in the grass.

"Disgusting," Phoebe said, pinching her face together.

Caroline tore off a piece of watermelon and made sure there weren't any seeds. She handed it to Phoebe.

"Yummy," Phoebe said. The pink juice dripped down her chubby chin.

The table Aunt June had set up in the yard was still full of food. Fried chicken legs, biscuits, hard-boiled eggs, vegetables, fruits, pies, and lemonade. They'd all eaten so much, and yet had plenty left.

Caroline handed Phoebe the rest of her watermelon. She was too full to take another bite. She moved and sat on the Growing Rock, next to Papa.

"I ate too much," she said, rubbing her belly.

Papa looked up at the stars. "We have a lot to be thankful for. That's for sure."

Caroline looked around. The boys were playing baseball. The women sat by the food talking. Blanche was off walking with Robert. Phoebe made a tent with Peter's little sisters. They climbed inside with their dolls and finished their food, pretending to be mamas cooking.

Soon, when the sky was even darker, they'd gather together and shoot firecrackers.

Papa seemed solemn, sitting there looking at the sky, thinking some kind of grown-up thoughts that didn't make sense. Not when it was a day to have fun.

"What's wrong, Papa?"

He sighed. "This Depression has changed things for a lot of folks. It's going to get worse before it gets better."

Why was Papa talking about that right now? When everyone was laughing and having a good time? The Depression was far, far away from Ripley. It was in those big cities that they read about in the paper. Not here, in such a small place, away from everything. Not here, where they grew their own food. Even their own Fourth of July watermelons. They'd never go hungry. They'd never have a hard time like people in big cities.

No, the Depression was something far away. Something President Hoover talked about on the radio, something adults worried about for no reason when they lived in Ripley.

Caroline snuggled close to Papa. He wrapped his arm around her and gave her a small squeeze.

"I'm sorry. I shouldn't be worrying about that now, I guess. We should just enjoy right now."

Caroline smiled. That was right. No use worrying about that now.

George and Peter ran toward her.

"Caroline, we're gonna start the fireworks in a second!" Peter said.

Papa moved his arm and grinned down at her. "Go on. Have some fun. Don't worry about a thing, Sweet Pea."

Caroline kissed him on the cheek. His unshaven face tickled her lips.

Papa smiled—but was he still worried?

No, he couldn't be.

She jumped off the Rock and ran to catch up with the others.

There were no lights in the sky this year. It was as if the holiday hadn't even come. Was she the only one who remembered what day it was?

Probably.

Aunt Elsmere had been with Phoebe all day long, trying to get her to eat and to ease her pain. Doctor Reynold said the pneumonia was now fully gone. But Phoebe was so weak and thin, it would be several months before she'd gain her strength back.

It was hard to believe Blanche had been gone almost two days already. By now, they'd be well situated with Kenneth's family. Had Blanche changed any? In two days, how much could an expecting lady's belly grow?

Caroline rubbed her own stomach. It felt sore and tight. Not as if she was going to throw up, but tense and irritated. Her face dripped with saltiness. The window was open, like always, but that hardly made any difference.

July had arrived with a heated hatred that burned with no mercy.

She raised the nightgown up over her head and pulled her arms out of the sleeves. Her stomach poked out a little bit, bloated like it did sometimes from eating the wrong thing. Her chest felt sore, too. She stared down at her body, with her chin touching her collar bone. It seemed a tiny bit fuller at the top.

Good.

Maybe she was growing.

The sheets felt wet. Not wet with sweat, but wet and sticky. A thicker kind of wetness. She moved her arms toward her. Bare skin. Warmth rose to her face. She'd fallen asleep with nothing on, except her panties. Not that that mattered, since she was the only girl in there tonight, but, still.

Caroline reached for her nightgown. Her hand got some of the wetness on it.

It was a dark wetness. She squinted in the dark and lit the candle.

It was red. Several small spots of pink were splattered on the sheets. Pink lined the fingers she used to touch it. She stood up. One larger, darker stain had been underneath her.

It was too bad Blanche wasn't there. Mama wouldn't be any help. Aunt Elsmere was asleep. She took the candle and searched the dresser. Blanche hadn't taken everything with her. A few of her rags, old and stained, but cleaned, were still there.

Caroline put on a fresh pair of panties and folded a rag inside it the best she could. Then she put the nightgown back on.

The sheets looked soiled. Maybe it would be better to sleep on the cot on the porch until she could see to clean the sheets in the morning.

She tiptoed with the candle, but when she got on the porch, she didn't stop at the cot. Instead she walked all the way outside, though it didn't feel much cooler. She sat on the Growing Rock, tucking her legs underneath her.

Had it only been a few years ago since she'd sat there with Papa, thinking none of the Depression would affect them?

She felt like laughing. How stilly and childish that had been. Of course, she *had* been a child then. They'd all been younger and happier then.

Now they were separated, and Mama wasn't cutting watermelon or smiling, or doing much of anything. Peter was alive, but now everything had changed between them. What if Peter had been in so much pain that he hadn't meant what he said the other day? How could he want to be with her and all of her problems, when he could be spending his time with girls like Anna?

Caroline felt the tears start. She hadn't really cried since the accident—not even when Blanche left—but it was as if her body had forgotten all about that. Once she started, it felt good. She couldn't stop. Her whole body shook. She clenched her stomach in her hands.

How it hurt—becoming a woman. She'd wanted to grow up so bad, but why'd it have to hurt that much?

Why did Papa have to leave? Why did Blanche have to get married? Why did Robert have to feel so alone and kill himself? Why did Phoebe have to be sick? Why did George have to disappear? Why wasn't Mama ever there for her?

Why, on top of everything else, did Amelia Earhart's plane have to go missing a couple of days before? Her hero—was she gone like George? Did the thing that brought her so much happiness—flying—also bring her death?

Robert's funeral had been that afternoon. A small, private family funeral with a closed coffin lid. Only a week before, everyone had planned on being family with Robert. Now, not one of them was even invited to his funeral. No one had gotten to say goodbye.

It hurt—to care about people, and to live and to grow. She cried for all of these things.

And, then, all of a sudden, she quit.

Someone had heard. Someone had made the grass move and the dried leaves rustle.

Someone had heard her and come outside.

Caroline tried wiping her face on her nightgown sleeve, but it was too late.

Mama stood there, pale and thin, staring at her.

Caroline wiped her face. "It's—it's okay. There's nothing wrong. I just have a stomach ache."

Mama sat on the Rock beside her. "I'm sorry," she whispered. "I'm so, so sorry."

"Sorry for what?"

"Sorry for not being here for my children the way I should have been. The way I need to be." Mama rocked her body in forward motion, as if she were sitting in her rocker. "It could have been one of my children who got shot."

Caroline breathed deeply. Neither of them said anything for a long time. The crickets chirped.

She patted Mama's arm. All summer, it had been easy to be mad at her. To feel angry and frustrated when Papa was gone and there'd been plenty of work to do. Now, it made sense why Mama felt so bad all the time. It made sense now why people sometimes shut doors when things felt hopeless.

"Mama, I love you."

Mama pulled her closer and kissed the top of her head, the way she did when she'd been a little girl. "I love you too. I love all of you."

The words felt good and soothing, as if they were wrapping themselves around Caroline and making the hurt go away. She could never get sick of hearing those words.

Mama didn't say anything else, but she seemed a little different. After all, she was eating a tiny bit more and going outside lately.

Was she finally coming out of that secret place, that awful way of thinking that she seemed to go to more and more often? Was she going to get back to normal, the way she did after Phoebe was born? Or the way she had after Thomas married and moved a few miles away?

They sat there a long time, looking up at the stars.

They walked hand-in-hand to the back porch just as the sky grew lighter.

"Caroline," Phoebe held the kitten in her arms, rocking it back and forth. "What's the kitty's name?"

"Hmm."

She hadn't even thought about what to name it. Maybe it was because Papa always said not to name their farm animals. When they'd had a lot—now there were just some chickens, and no horses or mules or pigs like before. But this kitten was different. They wouldn't be eating it.

The kitten licked Phoebe's arm, and she giggled. She pulled a piece of blue yarn from the basket beside her bed and held it up in the air, right above the kitten's head. It bounced on its hind legs and swatted its paws at the yarn, trying to catch it.

The kitten seemed to like Phoebe better than it liked Caroline. Oh, well. She couldn't blame it. Phoebe had more patience and played with it more.

"Why don't you name it? I don't have any good ideas."

Phoebe's eyes widened. "Hmm. Let me think a minute."

She pulled some string out of her basket, threaded a needle, and began stitching a hole on Aunt Elsmere's apron.

Phoebe couldn't even read yet, but during all the time she'd spent in bed, she'd learned how to sew and mend, and her hand was almost as steady as Mama's. It was something

Caroline and Blanche had never been very good at it.

Maybe Caroline would bring Phoebe and the kitten along to Miss Evelyn's one day, and Phoebe could fix all of those socks that needed mending before winter.

"Felix," Phoebe said, all of a sudden, not taking her eyes away from the apron.

"Felix?"

"Yep." Phoebe sighed. "Now all we need is a goose. One that lays golden eggs!"

Oh, of course. Felix the Cat. Robert had treated Phoebe to a movie one day sometime the year before, and the cartoon at the beginning was "Felix the Cat and the Goose That Laid the Golden Egg." Phoebe had talked about it and drawn pictures in Caroline's school book.

"Good pick. Felix the Cat, it is."

Phoebe smiled. Felix jumped on the apron and tried biting the thread out of her hand.

Chapter 19

Caroline carried several small rags to wipe herself off. Papa's hat fell over her eyes, and she pushed it back so she could see the plants before her. She tucked the damp wisps of hair coming out of her braid behind her ears.

It was hard to tell sometimes which was the baby cotton plant and which was the weed. But, already, the cotton plants had their first little, white flower blossoms. These would change colors, and then, soon, the bolls would open, and there would be a sea of whiteness. She leaned over and chopped several large weeds with the garden hoe. She pushed them away from the cotton plant, giving it room to grow.

She hoped Papa would be home soon, and they'd be able to get a few hired hands like normal. They probably wouldn't be able afford as many as before, especially with the crop being smaller, but it would still be a decent year, even though they planted later than before.

After all, for the last week, Caroline had hardly done anything except work out in the fields with Uncle P. Joe and Aunt June, and Thomas whenever he could be there, chopping cotton. Around the beginning of October, they'd begin the picking season. If Papa had the money to get mules or horses. Otherwise, how would they ever transport those heavy sacks of cotton to the cotton gin? Would all their weeks of harvesting be a waste?

Someone's hand slipped over Caroline's eyes.

"Guess who?" Peter asked.

Caroline giggled and turned around.

Peter popped a piece of peppermint candy in her mouth before she could say anything.

She moved the candy to the side of her jaw with her tongue. "Well, hello." She wiped her hands on her towel. "You comin' to join in on this fun today?"

"You betchya." Peter took the hoe out of her hands and started chopping. He never wasted a minute. He'd talk, but the whole time, he'd be working.

Caroline sucked on the yummy peppermint and watched Peter's strong arms and shoulders move quickly. His bandage was gone, and now there was just a deep scar that you wouldn't know was there unless his shirt was off.

Peter turned around, his face already damp looking. "Well, ain't you gonna help? Can't stand there all day and let me do the work." He grinned and tossed a long weed at her.

Caroline slapped his arm with her sweaty cloth.

Soon, Doctor Reynold said Phoebe's lungs were out of danger. As long as she was careful not to breathe in dust, or over-exhaust herself, she would be fine, even though he still dropped by once a week or so to check on her.

Aunt Elsmere and Mama let Phoebe do whatever she wanted inside the house, but they were strict on where she went and what she did. Any germs or anything at all that could upset her breathing could make her very sick again.

At first, Phoebe seemed thankful to get out of her room. But playing in the hot house with Felix became dull in no time. She'd mended just about everything there was that needed to be fixed in that house, and she'd patched up lots of things Caroline brought from Miss Evelyn's too—it would be a while before she'd get to go to her dusty house and meet her.

"Can I go play with Annie and Debra Jean?" she asked probably a dozen times a day.

"No, but maybe soon. Eat up and gain some weight and get some strength back, and you'll be well enough to go to school this fall," Aunt Elsmere would say, trying to get her to eat some cake or cornbread, or something rich that would "stick to her bones."

School.

Now that August was approaching soon, school wasn't too far away anymore. Maybe Phoebe would actually get to go, after all.

One day when it was too hot to get much work done, Caroline and Peter came inside to see Phoebe. Not even that cheered her up, though, and she whined so much, Aunt Elsmere sent them all outside with a cookie each and lemonade.

"I'm tired of not getting to do anything." Phoebe clutched the kitten in her lap and rocked the swing back and forth. It still squeaked awfully loud.

"I know how you feel. When I was hurt, I stayed inside a lot too," Peter said.

"But not *after* you started feeling better." Phoebe crammed her entire cookie in her mouth at once. When she finished chewing, she gulped down half a glass of lemonade. "I'm eating everything so I can get fat and go play with Annie and Debra Jean."

Peter laughed.

Caroline wanted to, but she didn't because of the frown on Phoebe's face.

"It's not funny."

"We know," Caroline said. "But don't worry. Soon, you'll get to leave the house every day for school."

"But that won't be much fun. I'm going on eight, and I'll be the only one who can't read." Phoebe crossed her arms and squished Felix. He jumped from her arms and went to sit beneath the porch.

Phoebe was right. She probably wouldn't be the only one, but there were lots of kids her age who'd been in school a year or longer.

Maybe if they started working with her now, Phoebe would be caught up a little bit, at least enough to go to the first grade class. She already knew her alphabet. Reading was like sewing—just a matter of putting all the letters together.

"I'll be right back," Caroline said.

She ran inside to get some paper and a pencil and a couple of her books.

"What are you doing in here? You can't come in if you're gonna whine." Aunt Elsmere stuck her head from the kitchen and shook a big spoon.

"It's just me." Caroline got what she needed from the secretary desk. "Peter and I are going to help Phoebe learn how to read and write."

"Humph. Good. I just hope she doesn't bury her head in a book all the time the way you do."

Caroline didn't answer.

Reading was often the best thing to do if you were trapped inside the house with Aunt Elsmere all day.

Amelia Earhart was still missing. That story had been on the front page of the paper for a while. A black and white Amelia stared up at Caroline with her short, curly head of hair, standing in front of her plane and looking happy.

Caroline skimmed the article with a sinking heart. How was it that people could just go missing? How could anyone disappear like that?

She flipped through the rest of the mail Thomas had brought over. A pale pink envelope with curly writing she'd know anywhere was addressed to her.

Thomas grinned at her from his place at the table next to Mama. He recognized the writing too, but he didn't say anything.

Maybe he understood she wanted to read the letter alone. After all, she never received anything addressed just to *her*.

She ran outside and sat under the oak tree.

Dear Caroline,

This seems so silly—never thought I'd have to write to you. Actually, I never thought I'd get out of Ripley, but, here I am, in a different state. This is better than I thought. Kenneth's family is all very sweet (they think I got pregnant after we married), but I don't know them well yet, so I feel awkwerd all the time. I didn't realize that I don't know Kenneth that well yet either. I didn't know he's terible at hunting. I didn't know he finished school at the top of his class. I didn't know he doesn't like jam—on anything. It makes me feel sad I have so much to learn about him and his family. But one thing is for sure—I love him more than ever. We dined at a nice restarant in town last night and we may go see a movie in the next couple of weeks. You know I'm always dying to go do things.

Kenneth's sisters are dears. Louise is nineteen but she acts younger than me. Tulip just turned sixteen. I think you'd like her. She's a bit of a tomboy and loves to be outside. His mother waits on me hand and foot and says I need to take care of myself. I don't have to work and sweat the way I always had to at home. They were all appalled when I told them how we womenfolk had to labor away in the fields. So I just sit around all day eating whatever I please while Kenneth works for his father—he owns a car company. Guess that's why he drives such a nice car. All the other businesses shut down when the Depression hit, but not theirs. Their business always seems to be booming—my husband comes from a talented group!

Though it hasn't been long, I feel like it's been ages, sweet Caroline. How will I ever get through these trying months ahead without you and Phoebe? Please give everyone my love, and write when you can.

Lots of hugs,
Blanche

Caroline grinned. The letter was so—Blanche. Even the floral stationary. She could see Kenneth's family now, waiting on Blanche all the time, hovering around her the way Aunt Elsmere always did. How long would it take for them to see the real Blanche?

She leaned back against the tree trunk. The real Blanche would probably not write Caroline all the time. Once she made friends and grew to know Kenneth's family more, the letters would become more and more rare. She'd make up excuses about being busy and not feeling well and wouldn't write as often.

But maybe that was the old Blanche. Maybe she'd changed.

May and June had been filled with one thing after another—good and bad things. July was mainly composed of nothings—not nothing, of course, but sameness. Every day, Caroline worked outside, while Aunt Elsmere did the inside jobs, though Mama had started doing small things here and there, like cleaning dishes or putting bread in the oven. Mama still didn't talk that much, but Phoebe chattered away and forced her to talk.

Every day, Caroline worked with Peter. Then they took an afternoon break and practiced reading and writing with Phoebe. She'd be so worn out, she'd usually go to bed after supper.

It had all grown to be the same, once Blanche left and once Phoebe was well again.

Caroline tossed on the cot. Tomorrow was the start of August—the start of more sameness.

Peter's house was dark. If they used their lights, she would have been able to spot a dot of light in the distance. He must've been asleep.

Too bad she wasn't. It was one of those nights she felt too restless to sleep in her room.

Something moved in the bushes. Felix purred at the screened-in door.

"What is it, boy?"

He kept purring. He scratched the screen with his paws.

That time she heard it. Something had moved in the bushes. Then it sounded as if someone was walking around inside the house. Caroline lit her candle and walked inside. Felix followed her.

"What the—ouch," someone muttered.

Felix yelped and ran away.

"Who's there?" Caroline stepped past the kitchen and into the sitting room. Her heart pounded, and she picked up a candle holder. It wasn't much, but she needed something to defend herself.

The dark figure turned around just as the light touched reached its face. She dropped the candle, but the person caught it, burning two of his fingers.

George.

Caroline's heart sped up, and her whole body trembled.

Was this a dream? She tried pinching the sides of her legs. She was numb with disbelief.

George—older and thinner and hairier—but it was George—George—stood there staring at her. He held his burnt fingers to his chest. The candle was somehow still going. He'd set it on the secretary.

"Lord, you're not a little girl anymore."

Her feeling started coming back. She could breathe again. Should she cry or laugh? Be mad or happy?

She rushed over and hugged him, almost knocking him down.

"They thought you were dead. They all thought you were dead. Everyone did. Except me."

"I know. I'm sorry," George mumbled. He led her outside. "Let's not wake everyone yet."

Caroline followed, holding onto his arm, as if he might disappear again. When they stepped outside, not on the porch, but outside, between the house and the Growing Rock, she pulled away.

"Where the *hell* have you been? Do you have *any* idea how much we worried? Mama has gone crazy. She didn't eat. She didn't sleep. She thought you were *dead*. They all did. Except me."

George looked at her sadly, tiredly. His hair was still blonde under the moonlight, but he looked so much more grownup than he had months ago. He blew on his fingers to cool them off.

Caroline started crying. She hugged him again.

He was here. Months of worrying, nights of sleeplessness, and Mama—poor Mama. And, now, he was here.

She hiccupped into his shirt.

"Glad we're outside cause you would've woke everyone up with your loud mouth." He grinned.

Good ole George.

Caroline giggled. Then she turned serious again and let go. "*Where* have you been?"

"Maybe you should ask where have I *not* been." George ran a hand through his hair. He pulled on his suspenders with his other hand.

"Okay, where have you not been?" Caroline moved and sat underneath the oak tree.

"It's a long story."

"Well, do you think I can go to bed now? After this?"

"Well, before I left here, I told y'all I was going to go find work, but I left out some of my plan. I only told Robert—"

"George, do you—I guess you don't know—"

"That he's dead?" George said in almost a whisper. "Yeah. I know. I came by his house yesterday on my way here. Would've been here sooner, but that delayed me a bit. Stayed with his folks last night. Would've been here sooner, but I slept so blasted long—lost track of time."

Caroline nodded.

George sighed. He picked up a leaf and crushed it in between his fingers. Even in the moonlight, there were two big pink splotches on his thumb and index finger from the candle.

"Anyway, I had told Robert before—that I was going to go to the Memphis area a while, like I said, and then I was going to try my luck ridin' the rails."

Riding the rails? Sneaking on trains without paying and going somewhere for free? Like the hobos did?

And Robert had *known*? Why hadn't he said anything? Caroline had even thought of asking Robert if he'd had any ideas—oh, why hadn't she?

"Don't give me that look. I know it's a dumb idea, but I heard so many stories of people gettin' to better places that way, fast and easy. Stories of people my age and younger going to places up north, or places like California that had projects like that Golden Gate Bridge. Hundreds got jobs from that."

"So you made Robert promise not to say anything? Why didn't you write? Mama was just about sick to her stomach."

George put his hands over his face for a second. "Robert didn't know nothing else. He probably thought I was dead too."

"Well, where the blasted hell *were* you?"

George grinned. "Geez—I'm gone half a year, and I come

home, and my favorite lil sister's grown a foot and cussing like a sailor."

"Sorry—where were you?"

George looked up at the tree branches and avoided her face.

"Jail," he said. "I've been in jail. And won't Aunt Elsmere and Mama be thrilled about *that*? I went through a bunch of different places. I was nearly going back to Chicago a second time when I got caught—me and dozens of others. And I was put in jail. I wasn't released till last week."

Which was why he hadn't written. Which was why no one had heard anything about him. Maybe that was why he looked so tired and pale.

George finally looked at her.

"I thought when I went away, I could make things better. But I didn't. I came back, and Robert's dead. I guess Blanche is gone?"

Caroline nodded.

"Well—good. I'm not ready to see her yet. I need to—get used to this first." He sat there, silent.

"I'm glad you're back, George. I *knew* you were coming back."

George put his arm around her. "I knew you would, sis. I knew I could count on you to figure I'd done something stupid and would come home." They walked back to the house.

"Lord, you've grown."

Good ole George.

Chapter 20

Mama was hysterical.

She cried and laughed, then cried again. Aunt Elsmere stood in the doorway behind her, pale as if she'd seen a ghost. Phoebe bounced up and down, holding onto George's hand.

"Caroline knew you were coming. When I got sad, she told me about the Growing Rock, and I think she knew the whole time you were coming back!"

It had never felt so loud in that hot, crowded kitchen before. Caroline had been sitting in there with George while he ate some breakfast when Aunt Elsmere had come downstairs.

She stared at him for the longest time. The first thing she said was, "Does your mama know yet?"

Then Aunt Elsmere had gone to wake Mama up and give her the news, gently as she could. "She'll have a heart attack if she just walks in and sees him like I did. That's enough to make a body crazy."

But Mama still acted crazy. She asked George a million questions, and when he tried to answer them, she hugged or kissed him or asked another question and kept saying, "I can't believe you're here."

Even when Phoebe started having a cough attack, Mama didn't take her eyes away from George. Aunt Elsmere patted Phoebe on the back and poured some cough syrup in the blue wooden spoon Aunt June had painted just for Phoebe to take her medicine.

Caroline grinned at George. His oatmeal now sat there, cold, because he hadn't touched it once they'd all come downstairs.

George grinned back at her as Mama cried some more and Phoebe gulped the cough syrup down, then climbed on the chair, begging for a piggy back ride, the kind he always used to give.

Caroline stepped outside on the screened porch and walked down the hill to meet Peter.

She only glanced back twice.

"George—is home," were the first words Caroline said when she saw Miss Evelyn. It was the first thing she'd said to everyone she saw in the last couple of days.

"Wonder how long he'll stay this time," Miss Evelyn said. "That's great news."

Caroline shrugged. "Probably forever." He was back, he was there now, so that's all that mattered.

"Where's the kitten you keep promising to bring?"

"Sorry. He's with Phoebe. She gets mad every time I come here cause Mama and Aunt Elsmere won't let her leave. She's always jealous when I go anywhere, so I let her watch him."

Miss Evelyn nodded. "Nothing like a pet for a lonely soul." She picked up her orange cat and rubbed him behind his ears.

Caroline felt awkward all of a sudden. Miss Evelyn was lonely—anyone could see it. It made her feel bad when she thought about how much she hated going there at first. Maybe when she got home, she'd ask if Miss Evelyn could come to supper soon.

"What do you want me to do today?"

Miss Evelyn motioned toward the empty chair next to hers. "I can't keep enough projects. You come by lots more than the church said when they told me they'd send someone to help. So, nothing. No work today. It's too hot anyhow." She looked around. "And my husband's been sending spies on me and the children. They may be watching us, so let's stay here. How about we just talk?"

It had been like that a lot lately. It seemed like Miss Evelyn's husband had been coming by more and more recently, no matter how long ago he died.

Caroline opened up her bag and pulled several books out. "What would you like to read today?"

George was different.

Of course he would be—he'd been gone a long time. Of course, he'd have changed somehow.

But he had changed more than Caroline would've ever thought.

They picked tomatoes silently. The only noises were ones made from pulling the tomatoes, or their baskets brushing against the tomato plants

After the first couple of days, George grew solemn. He didn't laugh over everything or wear that mischievous grin all the time like he once had. Now, he seemed to be thinking an awful lot, almost worried looking, with his blonde eyebrows arched in a frown.

Caroline started pulling another tomato, but paused. It was too green still. She sighed.

Stupid tomatoes.

"George. Tell me about the places you went and the people you met."

His face lit up for a second. "When I left Mississippi, I went through Alabama, and stayed in Atlanta a few days. I came back through Tennessee, caught a train to Ohio, and from there I went through Indiana and then Chicago. I was in St. Louis, trying to get on another train and go back the way I'd come, go back to Chicago, when—when we all got caught."

"What was jail like?"

George's face clouded over. "Hell. For one, knowing y'all were worrying about me was the worst feeling. Second, I had no way to tell anyone where I was. Oh, we could get calls, but no one knew where I was, so you wouldn't be calling me. I would've called y'all, but there ain't a phone here. I didn't know Aunt June's number. I never used it before. Hadn't needed to."

George pulled a huge tomato and put in one of the empty baskets. Two full baskets, and two empty ones left.

"Riding those trains was something else, though. You know that excited feeling you get right before you jump in the pond? Or like the time we snuck in the Bisbee Show? It's kinda like that, only stronger. And I went to so many places, in just a matter of a few weeks. Trying not to get caught is fun until you're caught. But jail was hell. Just miserable. I was with some people who really needed to be there."

Caroline shivered. "Well, at least you're home now."

George didn't say anything. Again, like his letters, he'd hardly described anything at all. He'd only given the small details. Details that didn't tell her anything, really.

He wore that solemn look again. With his clean-shaven face, she could see his cheek bones sticking out from where he'd clenched his teeth.

Maybe he kept thinking about Robert too.

Aunt June and Uncle P. Joe, Thomas and Pamelia, and Peter stayed for supper that night. It was the entire family, except for Papa and Blanche.

Mama sat by George and kept smiling at everyone, all together. She ate everything on her plate and even got up for seconds.

Their kitchen table wasn't large enough to seat everyone, so Caroline, Peter, and Phoebe ate at their own fold-up table George had brought down from the attic.

The door to the porch stood open, letting in a bit of a

breeze. In a couple of weeks, it'd probably start getting cooler. They all hoped that the hottest part of the year had passed, in time for them to pick cotton.

"I can read pretty good now," Phoebe said. "I read a verse in Aunt June's Bible today."

Peter took a big bite of fried chicken. "Proud of you. We'll be in school in just a few weeks. By September."

Caroline spooned her mashed potatoes. Just a few more weeks. She'd been worried they wouldn't get to go to school—how could they with so much work to do? But Aunt Elsmere said the other day that that was against the law, and they had to go. And now with George around, there was at least one extra person home.

"Whatchya kids up to over here? Why wasn't I invited to sit at the fun table?" Aunt June squatted down next to Phoebe and kissed her on the cheek.

She glanced at Peter and then at Caroline and winked.

Caroline's face turned red.

Aunt June acted as if she hadn't done anything. Peter was too busy eating his cornbread to notice.

"I made a cake," Aunt June whispered, her red curls tickling Phoebe's face.

"Oh, goodie! What kind?" Phoebe asked, clapping her hands together.

"A big cherry chocolate cake. George's favorite, now that he's back." She shook her head and stared at the table. "I can't believe he's home. I don't think I'll be used to it for a while."

Caroline turned around in her seat to look too. The sun was just setting, and an orange light streamed in around them. They all ate and talked. Mama looked prettier than she'd ever looked before—even prettier than she had in that wedding photo.

Radiant like the sun.

After supper, everyone else left, but Peter stayed around a while. He sat with Caroline on the front porch. She held Felix in her lap.

"He seems bigger every time I see him," Peter said, stroking his head.

"I guess he is."

It was easier for Peter to notice. He didn't always see Felix every day the way she did. But looking at him, it was definitely true that he'd grown a lot. Felix the cat was almost just that—a cat, not a kitten anymore.

"Any new word from Blanche?" Peter asked.

"Nah, not yet."

Inside, Aunt Elsmere was banging dishes around, telling George he needed to start doing more to help around the house.

"You could do dishes once and while, you know."

"Why can't I go outside too?" Phoebe wailed.

"Because Caroline is spending time with Peter."

"So? Why can't I be with them?"

"Because Caroline and Peter may be more than friends," Mama said, gently.

"Like Blanche and Robert?"

"Let's talk about something else," Aunt Elsmere said. "Here, eat another piece of cake."

"Do you—do you wanna go for a walk?" Peter asked.

Thank goodness. The family could be quite embarrassing sometimes. "Sure."

As they got up, Peter almost tripped on the top step. "Geez, it's dark."

There wasn't any moon shining tonight. It hid behind the clouds, as if it was going to rain.

"Remember when we were little, and we used to make our own lights by collecting lighting bugs?" Caroline reached her hand out and grabbed one. The bug squirmed beneath her fingers. It glowed, making her skin look pink.

Peter grinned. He picked up the Mason jelly jar he'd used to drink water in that afternoon, still sitting on the porch. "Want to do that again?"

He held her hand and carried the jar by its top with his other hand, his palm covering the lid so the bugs wouldn't escape.

"Sorry about—well—about them talking in there about you. About us."

Peter let go of her hand for a minute and caught another bug. "It's okay. I mean, I figured somebody would start saying something sometime."

Caroline nodded, but didn't look at him. The jar was already full of a bright glow, but she stared ahead, searching for more lightning bugs.

"I'm okay with it if you are," she said, "It doesn't bother me if they wanna say that—or if it's true."

Peter took her hand again.

After a few more minutes, their jar was pretty full.

"It feels like they're attacking my hand."

"Let's go ahead and let them go then."

They bent down on the ground, and Caroline pulled Peter's hand away from the jar.

It had always been her favorite part, watching the bugs fly away. It was as if the sky was full of fairies that had come out from the Growing Rock. Maybe some of them actually were fairies, and they just didn't know it. Maybe if Phoebe was looking out of the bedroom window, she'd see them.

Peter wasn't even watching the bugs fly off.

This time Caroline held his hand first.

He moved closer to her, close enough that she could see the freckles on his nose, even in the darkness. It was so close, her sunburn seemed to tingle more.

It happened so fast, she didn't have time to be scared. But even if she'd had time to think, she wouldn't have been scared anyway. Because it was the perfect time. Because it felt right.

He kissed her.

And this time, they both understood what was special about it.

Chapter 21

"You won't believe who I talked to," Mama said. She set down the bag full of sugar and flour, and whatever else she'd gotten at the store.

It was good that she'd left the house and been gone all morning and most of the afternoon.

"Who?"

"Well, when I dropped Phoebe off at June's, she'd had it all planned."

"Had what planned?" Caroline opened the grocery sack and started putting things away.

Mama's face was bright pink. Her hair was falling from its bun, but she didn't bother fixing it. "She had it planned for my anniversary that I'd get to speak to *him*."

"To Papa?"

"Yes! She had him call just minutes after I got there, and that's why she'd insisted on me having Phoebe there right on time."

"Oh, Mama, that's great. How is he?"

"He was doing really well—ain't nothing like hearing his voice. I'm not much of one for writing letters, you know." She sat down at the table.

Caroline poured her a glass of water and dropped in a few of the last ice cubes that they'd bought from the ice man earlier. Mama wrapped her trembling hands around the glass.

"He said to tell you all he's coming home."

"When?"

"Soon. I'm not sure. He's not sure yet, but soon. He said it's been too hard being away from us. He hopes to be home in the next couple of weeks, if he can. He's saved more than enough for some good farm animals."

Soon.

The word was like cool water on a July day.

Soon.

"Amelia still hasn't shown up," George said. He slammed the paper down on the porch floor.

Caroline closed *Little Women*. "Maybe she's like you. Maybe she's okay, but just can't tell anyone."

"I swear, you're always so positive."

Caroline shrugged.

"Geez, it's hot." George slapped a mosquito that landed on his arm.

"Shush with all your complaining. It's much cooler than it's been. It's not so bad anymore."

"Yeah, I guess you're right. Guess I'll go in and help Aunt Elsmere start fixin' supper."

He opened the door. Aunt Elsmere was getting into it about something with Mama. "Geez, this woman's controlling. Leave for a few months, and she's moved in and taken over. Geez," George muttered as he went inside.

Caroline opened her book. She'd reached the part where the March sisters and Laurie were talking about building castles in the sky. It was one of her favorite parts, but she couldn't focus. She curled her legs up underneath her.

George wasn't going to stay.

They probably all knew it. It was easy to see on his restless face that he didn't want to stay in Ripley, that maybe he felt he didn't belong there. Not anymore, not after what had happened with Robert. Not after he'd gone and seen some of the world. Not after he'd changed.

It was only a matter of time before he said he was going somewhere else. Caroline wished he'd do it the right way when he did, not breaking the law this time. And that he wouldn't go too far away. She wanted him to wait a while after Papa returned, especially for Mama's sake.

Caroline sighed. The sky had a purplish tint to it, and the air was definitely cooler. She pushed against the back of the swing and made it move.

It screeched loudly. She'd meant to oil it all summer and still hadn't.

The first day of school was in the morning.

They were done chopping cotton. The flowers were deep red now, and they'd fall off any time. It was almost ready to pick. The days would soon be shorter, the nights would soon be much longer, and they'd be together more, no matter how sick or restless anyone got.

Maybe she'd come home from school one of these days soon, and Papa would be standing right here, waiting on them.

Or maybe Caroline would be sitting on the swing, not doing much of anything, and she'd see him, a growing speck in the distance.

Maybe tonight that would be the story she'd tell Phoebe—how they'd both stand up at the same time and wait to see Papa's face to make sure it was him before they took off. She'd give Phoebe her head start, like always, and then they'd run as fast as they could to meet him—like the Growing Rock's fairies, ready to fly.

Acknowledgements

The Growing Rock is a piece of fiction, but the setting of the book, the historical events referenced throughout it, and the emotions and hardships of the characters are all very real. There are characteristics of myself and those around me buried within these people on the page. Just as Caroline's coming-of-age story wouldn't be possible without the complex dynamics within her family, this book wouldn't be what it is today without the collaboration of many individuals who have played important roles in my life.

Thank you to my grandparents, Ruby and Clarence, who told me the stories that initially inspired this book. I am forever grateful for the memories they kept alive by telling them to me and for answering the never-ending questions I always had about their childhoods. The book would not be what it is without all of the rich details that they provided about growing up in the 1930s. I miss my grandpa greatly, and I regret that he did not ever get to see the final manuscript. The love he showed for my grandma and their 69 years of marriage has had a huge impact on my life, and I am thankful for having known such a strong, loving person.

I'm extremely grateful for the influence that the rest of my family has had upon my writing. Ever since I learned the alphabet, my parents have fed my hunger to read and learn, and they introduced me to books that remain some of my favorites. I will always appreciate the many trips to the library and their reading drafts of my work, proofreading, editing, and being honest with me. Thank you to my two sisters and two brothers, whose friendship and sibling rivalries helped me create the relationships between Caroline and her own siblings.

A huge shout out goes to those I had the honor to meet during my time as a graduate student at Lesley University. Thank you to Susan Goodman and Pat Lowery Collins, who served as my mentors for this book. They both not only helped me with the craft of writing, but they also pushed me to levels I had never been as a writer. Even after I graduated, they continued to offer me advice and encouragement. Thank you to Sabrina Fedel and Cynthia Platt for being cheerleaders for me throughout the publication process. Thank you to those I had in class workshops, and, of course, thank you to the Lesley Posse.

Thank you to Harvard Square Editions for giving Caroline's story a home in the literary world and helping me turn my greatest dream into a reality. Thank you to Jeff Guy for creating such a lovely cover that captures Caroline's world.

A heartfelt thank you goes to my husband, Kyle. I would not be the person I am today, and I may not have ever achieved this goal if I didn't have him in my life. He wouldn't let me give up on Caroline's story, and when I felt hopeless, he reminded me of why I needed to keep going. He and our Yorkie named Boston patiently listened to idea after idea as revision after revision took place, and words can't express what that means to me.

Lastly, many, many thanks to the readers of this book. No matter where you live or how old you are, this book is for you. *The Growing Rock* will always have a very special place in my heart. In many ways, I grew along with Caroline as I wrote it. Thank you for sharing in her struggles and joys and letting this story become part of your own life.

More books from Harvard Square Editions

People and Peppers, Kelvin Christopher James

Dark Lady of Hollywood, Diane Haithman

Gates of Eden, Charles Degelman

Living Treasures, Yang Huang

Close, Erika Raskin

Anomie, Jeff Lockwood

Nature's Confession, J.L. Morin

Love's Affliction, Dr. Fidelis O. Mkparu

Fugue for the Right Hand, Michele Tolela Myers

A Little Something, Richard Haddaway

Growing Up White, James P. Stobaugh

Calling the Dead, R.K. Marfurt

Parallel, Sharon Erby

www.ingramcontent.com/pod-product-compliance
Lightning Source LLC
Chambersburg PA
CBHW031953010726
47493CB00007B/2184